THE HIMALAYAN RESCUE

Dave Gustaveson

YWAM
Publishing
A Ministry of Youth With A Mission
P.O. Box 55787, Seattle, WA 98155

YWAM Publishing is the publishing ministry of Youth With A Mission. Youth With A Mission (YWAM) is an international missionary organization of Christians from many denominations dedicated to presenting Jesus Christ to this generation. To this end, YWAM has focused its efforts in three main areas: 1) Training and equipping believers for their part in fulfilling the Great Commission (Matthew 28:19). 2) Personal evangelism. 3) Mercy ministry (medical and relief work).

For a free catalog of books and materials write or call:
YWAM Publishing
P.O. Box 55787, Seattle, WA 98155
(425) 771-1153 or (800) 922-2143
www.ywampublishing.com

The Himalayan Rescue

Copyright © 2000 by David Gustaveson

Published by Youth With A Mission Publishing
P.O. Box 55787
Seattle, WA 98155

ISBN 1-57658-027-X

Printed in the United States of America.

To my daughter Katie
on her fifteenth birthday
May the beauty of the Lord God
always shine upon you and keep you
as the apple of God's eye

Other

REEL KIDS
Adventures

Available at your local Christian bookstore or
YWAM Publishing
1-800-922-2143

Acknowledgments

Kids face trouble in a world gone wrong. This book tells the story of two children in real danger. God's heart breaks for a world in which over one hundred million abandoned kids struggle every day to survive on the streets.

No one can forget how the terror of gunfire shattered the lives of hundreds of students on a secure high school campus. Tragedies like the one in Littleton are becoming too familiar in our daily lives. Children are all too powerless, and we must look to a loving and powerful God for answers.

Our world grieves at the images of refugees and their weeping children who must flee the loss and pain of civil war. Worldwide exploitation of child labor causes us to question the real cost of some of our clothes.

My greatest hope is that those reading this book will dedicate their lives to helping hurting children. God's love is the only safe haven for kids, and we must take that love to children everywhere.

A very special thanks to Marty and Kelly Meyer for their many hours of help on this book. Their passion to help turn around a hurting world is making a difference. I appreciate their friendship, and I enjoyed drawing from their experience of trekking in Nepal.

Also, special thanks to John Davidson for his insights on Nepal. Thanks to Frank Ordaz for his captivating cover art, and to Sara Mike and Marit Holmgren for their diligent editorial work.

And I can't forget to thank all the faithful soldiers at YWAM Publishing who commit daily to extending God's kingdom through good books.

May God raise up, for such a time as this, those who will change the world for children everywhere.

Table of Contents

Chapter 1

Helpless in Kathmandu

What was that?"

Jeff Caldwell's pulse quickened. His blue eyes locked on to his younger sister's terrified brown eyes.

Bam! Bam! Bam!

"Somebody is trying to break in!" Mindy gasped, bolting from the bamboo couch where she had been resting.

Trembling, Jeff forced his gaze toward the sudden disturbance. The door rattled as if it were going to come off its hinges.

Jeff and Mindy crawled to a nearby window.

"He's going to break the door down," Jeff panicked, ducking out of sight.

Mindy caught a glimpse of the man outside the apartment. His dark eyes glared through old, crooked glasses. A full, dark beard almost hid his rotten front teeth.

Stealing another peek, Jeff saw the man hit a large wooden club against a screwdriver near the lock.

Whack! Whack! Whack! The pounding sent chills up and down Jeff's spine. Mindy froze with fear as the door almost shook open.

Jeff's jet-lagged body stiffened. He rubbed his fingers nervously through his short, blond curls, praying as he had been since they first heard the pounding. His jeans and T-shirt stuck to his sweaty skin, and he suddenly felt too warm in his blue sweater. The hammering made him want to jump out of his new brown hiking boots.

"What are we going to do?" Mindy whispered. "We're all alone."

Jeff didn't have an answer. He looked helplessly at his thirteen-year-old sister. Her flashing braces reflected the late afternoon sunlight shining through the window. She yanked at her pale yellow ponytail, as she usually did when she was upset. Her eyes hid behind the glare that reflected off her glasses.

"What do you think he wants?" Mindy wondered out loud.

Jeff took a deep breath, straining for a solution. "I don't know. He probably wants to steal something. He'll be inside in no time. We need to hide."

The pounding grew louder as Jeff and Mindy ran up the stairs to the apartment's second floor.

Jeff opened a door. "Hurry. Let's get in this closet."

Mindy followed, pulling the door shut. "I didn't give up my Christmas vacation to die in Nepal."

As they sat in darkness, Jeff tried to focus his thoughts. It was Sunday, December 13. For months, the Reel Kids Club had dreamed of trekking the Himalayan Mountains of Nepal. Now that dream was coming true. The next day they would begin an adventurous trek in that tiny Hindu nation, the home of Mount Everest and two hundred other mountain peaks towering at least twenty thousand feet high.

Jeff put his ear to the closet door. The banging had finally stopped. Mindy started to shake. She hadn't been feeling well, so Jeff had elected to stay home with her while the rest of the team went into downtown Kathmandu with Emil, their Nepalese host.

"Maybe he's gone," Mindy whispered, hugging her knees to her chest.

"I hope so. Are you feeling any better?"

"I think my fever is gone."

As they sat in tense stillness, Jeff thought about the struggle they were already in. The airline had misplaced Mindy's bag, and the team's trekking permits had been rejected. Jeff knew Mindy was discouraged. She had worked hard preparing for this trip. As the Reel Kids Club researcher, she had spent months studying the Himalayas. If she didn't get to see them, she would be so disappointed.

"I'm sorry all this is happening to you at once," Jeff said.

Mindy shrugged. "It's just that it always seems to happen this way. I've worked for months just getting in shape. My muscles are wiped from all the bike riding, running, and walking. First my luggage gets lost, then we can't get permits. On top of that, I get sick, and now some nut tries to break in."

"It'll work out," Jeff encouraged his sister. "You'll get to trek."

Suddenly, they heard footsteps in the upstairs hall. Mindy grabbed Jeff's arm. The glimmer of light framing the door allowed them to see only silhouettes of each other. As the footsteps came closer, Jeff regretted that he hadn't battled his fears and stopped the man from breaking in. But it was too late now. They could only sit still and pray and hope he wouldn't find them.

The seconds crawled by. They heard the man rummaging through drawers and cabinets. Clearly, he was looking for something.

Mindy gripped Jeff's arm even tighter. Jeff's heart was thumping in his chest. He hoped that the rest of the team would get home soon. Barely breathing, the two of them stayed absolutely still until they heard the man go downstairs.

"Maybe he's leaving," Jeff whispered.

"I hope so," Mindy said, still shaking. "I hope he didn't take anything. We should have done something."

"I feel awful. I feel like a wimp."

"Should we call the police?"

Jeff slowly opened the door. "I don't know if there's a phone upstairs."

A strange quiet filled the house.

"I think he's gone," Mindy said. "I want to get out of this crazy closet."

Jeff nodded. "Let's head downstairs. But we need to be careful."

They tumbled out of the cramped closet and slowly tiptoed their way down the stairs. Together they cautiously checked the other rooms. Approaching the kitchen, they both gasped when they saw the front door creaking open. There was no time to hide.

As the door opened wide, Mindy sighed with relief. "It's Emil and Warren."

Jeff's muscles relaxed and he took a deep breath as his best friend K.J. walked in with his camera slung over his shoulders.

"What happened to you guys?" K.J. asked, noticing their tense expressions.

"You have no idea," Mindy sighed.

Everyone listened as Jeff and Mindy tried to calmly explain what had happened.

Emil placed his arm around Mindy. "I'm sorry about this. It must have been a burglar. He sure did a good job on the front door."

"He went through a lot of stuff upstairs," Jeff said.

Emil looked around. "I'll have to check it out."

"I'll have a look outside," Warren volunteered.

Jeff watched Emil search the apartment he shared with his wife, Mary Anne, and their adopted daughter, Nima. Even though he had just met Emil, Jeff was already glad that Warren had chosen him as their trekking guide. Emil was Jeff's height with a rounded dark brown face, high cheekbones, and dark hair. His eyes were filled with warmth, and he was always smiling, which sent his mustache up and down. Around his waist was a broad leather belt with the famous crescent-shaped Gurka knife and sheath. He made his living as a trekking guide.

Mindy looked up at Emil, who was a full seven inches taller than she. "I'm glad you're all home. What took you guys so long?"

"I got some great footage of Kathmandu," K.J. said, pulling his camcorder out of the bag. "We visited the Royal Palace, Durbar Square, and a Hindu temple. I even got some shots of the famous Freak Street."

"What's that?" Jeff asked.

Mindy put up two fingers with each hand. "Peace, man. That's where the hippies hung out in the sixties."

K.J. nodded. "That place was cool. There are still a few hippies there. I wish you guys could have seen it."

"I would have loved to," Mindy said. "But I was in a closet, hiding from a crazy burglar."

"Well, I guess we all got to meet some 'freaks,'" K.J. smiled.

Jeff grinned at his best friend. K.J.'s full name was Kyle James Baxter, such a serious name for such a funny guy. He had the ability to make people laugh during tense situations. Even his clothes were amusing. His sweatshirt had a picture of some hikers hanging from a mountain ledge with the words "Hang in there, baby" written across the top.

K.J. was the team cameraman. At fourteen, he had already developed a unique talent for film, and he would film anything in sight, no matter how risky.

K.J. pulled out his comb, running it through his thick, dark hair. His dark eyes beamed. He hugged his camcorder as if it were his best friend. "I'm really ready for this trip. There's some awesome footage to shoot in the Himalayas."

"How can you be so confident we're going?" Mindy asked. "We don't even have our trekking permits, and Emil says they'll be hard to get."

"We'll get them," K.J. said. "I know it."

Jeff looked up the stairway. "I hope Emil finds out what that guy wanted."

As Mindy sat down to rest, Jeff looked out the window at the busy Kathmandu neighborhood. His mind swam as he recalled the past few days. The team had flown countless hours on Singapore Airlines from Los Angeles International Airport to Singapore and then to Dakka, Bangladesh. Exhausted from travel, they finally touched down in Kathmandu, Nepal, early Sunday morning.

Even though the travel was tiring, Jeff felt privileged to go on trips like this and was grateful that the Reel Kids Club gave him such exciting opportunities. He had heard about the club right after his family moved to Los Angeles and he enrolled in Baldwin Heights High School. He and his sister had always had a great interest in media, probably because they were influenced by their parents' careers. Their dad was an anchorman at a local television station, and their mom worked as a part-time news correspondent. Both parents were thrilled with the unique experiences the club provided.

The Reel Kids Club presented ways for kids to develop their media skills, travel, and share their faith at the same time. They met off-campus but had permission to use school equipment. The goal was to produce, from start to finish, videos of their adventures and then show them to youth groups at local churches. They wanted to inspire the churches to send out missions teams of their own. As head of their school communications department, Warren Russell had hit upon the idea for the club.

"Nothing unusual outside," Warren reported as he came back inside. "Where is Emil?"

"He's still checking upstairs," Jeff said. "Did you have any success today with the permits?"

Warren looked discouraged. "It doesn't look good. We'll have to be at the office first thing tomorrow morning. Emil contacted a friend who works for the government, but he wasn't able to help us."

"Any news on my hiking gear?" Mindy asked.

"Not much," Warren said. "Emil called the airline earlier. They think your bag got mixed up with luggage from another flight. Emil will make some more calls and try to borrow gear that fits you."

Jeff admired how calm Warren was. His soft brown eyes were always friendly and warm. He was only an inch taller than Jeff, and they had the same medium build. Even though he was in his early thirties, he looked young enough to be mistaken for one of his students. Adding to the confusion, he had given the group permission to call him by his first name when they were away from school. The Reel Kids Club was the love of his life. Together the team had biked in China, trekked up the Amazon River to a distant Indian tribe, sailed to Haiti, and traveled through the jungles of Vietnam.

Just then, Emil rushed down the stairs. "I think I solved the mystery of the intruder."

"Do you know who it was?" Jeff asked.

"No. But I know what he was after." Emil sat down on the bamboo couch, his hands trembling as he looked at the piece of paper he held.

"What's wrong?" Mindy asked.

"This note was left on our bed."

Jeff was too curious to wait. "What does it say?"

Emil wiped a tear from his eye. "A few months ago, we were told about the possibility of adopting two young children. Because of our Christian faith, some of the children's relatives have been totally against it. They don't want the kids, but they don't want us to have them either. One of them must have broken in. He was looking for the adoption papers."

"Did he find them?" Warren asked.

"No. We keep them in a security box at the bank. But he left this note. It says that since he is a Hindu, he refuses to allow the kids to be raised in a Christian family. He warns us not to pursue it any further. My wife will be heartbroken over this."

Jeff was confused now. "If you have the legal papers, why don't you have the kids?"

"We're waiting for the adoption to be final on January fifteenth. We're also waiting for word from their grandmother, who has been taking care of them but is getting too frail and sick. The rest of the family is too poor to take them. The kids' mother died three years ago."

"What about their father?" K.J. asked.

"Their dad is a drug user who abandoned them."

Just then, Emil's wife and daughter came in from outside laughing. Everything about Emil's wife, Mary Anne, was bright. The small-framed woman was dressed in a bright blouse and skirt. Her dark hair was nicely braided, and her rounded face and chestnut eyes radiated the love of God. Twelve-year-old Nima was a little shorter and very slender in her blue jeans, red plaid shirt, and brown hiking boots. In her shyness, she seemed to hide behind her mother in the room full of strangers. The whole family spoke English very well.

Mary Anne could tell right away that something was wrong. She looked to Emil for an explanation. Emil handed her the note, which both she and Nima read. Mary Anne began to cry. As Emil put his arm around his wife, Nima ran to her bedroom.

Jeff and the others looked at one another nervously, not knowing what to do.

After a little while, Mary Anne looked up through her tears. "I'm sorry. We have wanted more than anything else in the world to adopt these kids." She wiped her eyes. "We lost our children in an accident several years ago. It was devastating. About a year ago, we adopted Nima, and a few months after that we heard about Tenzing and Chandra."

Mary Anne began to weep again, and Mindy crossed the room to give her a hug.

"We want to add to our family," Emil explained, "but it has been hard for Nima to accept."

Mary Anne reached for a little photo album. "Here are some pictures of the kids. Tenzing is five, and Chandra is three."

She turned the pages, showing the team several pictures of the two small children being held by various people. Nobody was smiling, and Jeff couldn't help but notice how tiny and sickly the children looked.

❖❖❖❖❖❖❖

An hour later, the team sat with Emil in the large living room while Mary Anne talked with Nima. The basic bamboo furniture was spread out on plain wooden floors, and a few scenic pictures from Emil's mountain treks decorated the walls. There was nothing fancy about the apartment, but Jeff knew it was a home. Jeff overheard Emil discussing the trip with Warren. "Mind if I join you?" he asked.

Warren pointed to the couch. "Have a seat. We're discussing our schedule for tomorrow."

Jeff sat down, and Warren explained their plan. "We'll need to be up early to arrive at the permit office by eight. If a miracle happens, we'll take the bus to Pokhara."

Mindy chimed in from across the room. "What about my hiking gear?"

"I'm working on that," Emil said with an optimistic smile.

Just as he was about to explain, the phone rang. Emil spoke in Nepali for several minutes. Jeff hoped that he was talking to either the permit office or the airline. His hope for good news faded, however, as the look on Emil's face grew more and more concerned.

Finally, Emil hung up the phone and took a deep breath. "It's about the kids. It's urgent."

Everyone leaned in. "I have to change my plans," Emil announced. His eyes were moist as he took his seat on the couch. "That was another trekker who just came down the mountain. He told me the kids are in serious trouble if I don't get them immediately."

"What's wrong?" Mindy asked, wide-eyed.

"Their grandmother is ready to give the kids to us. Two of their uncles are in full agreement that they need a home like ours. They are even willing to help carry Tenzing and Chandra down from Muktinath. But the oldest uncle, Goray, is against us. He says he has a better plan, but my friend has heard he's pretty greedy and wants to make money."

"What do you mean?" K.J. asked.

"He'll probably sell the kids for child labor."

"Oh no!" Mindy cried. "We've got to rescue them."

Chapter 2

Wild Bus Ride

Can we go with you?" Mindy asked.

Everyone looked at Emil.

"It's not possible for you to come without trekking permits."

"But we want to help you," Jeff said.

"You'll be stopped at the first checkpoint."

"We don't care," Mindy insisted. "We have to help."

Emil was silent, deep in thought. "I don't have a choice," he said finally. "I need to leave first thing in the morning. My friend says that Goray is planning to take the kids soon. Even if the adoption isn't final, I still have the papers."

"We understand," Warren assured Emil. "The kids come first."

"Where will we get another guide?" K.J. asked.

"You'll have to hire someone."

"Please, Emil," Mindy pleaded. "There has to be a way we can help."

Jeff agreed. "It's no accident we're here."

"What do you mean?" Emil asked.

Jeff cleared his throat. "Didn't you say that Tenzing and Chandra are in Muktinath?"

Emil nodded.

"Well, that's the Hindu holy city. We could change our plans and hike with you. We wanted to do a video on the unreached people in Marpha. But I think God has a higher purpose." Jeff paused a moment. His eyes were wide with excitement, and he saw the same excitement mirrored in Warren's eyes, and in K.J.'s and Mindy's, too. Jeff's heart beat faster. "I believe God wants us to help rescue the kids. We could get the story on video."

Emil stood up, slowly scratching his head. "Maybe you're right. The hike we had planned is on the same route to Muktinath. I was really excited about Nima going with you. She's a good trekker." He rubbed his chin. "I'll make you a deal. We'll go to the office in the morning. If you get your permits, we'll go together. But keep in mind that the trip's main purpose is to rescue the kids."

Jeff slapped hands with K.J. and Mindy. "Yes!" they cheered.

Emil chuckled. Then his face grew serious. "Remember, if you don't get the permits, then I go alone."

"Let's have a prayer meeting tonight," Warren suggested. "God is bigger than that government office."

"What about my hiking gear?"

"I'll try to find some," Emil said. "Otherwise..."

"Otherwise what?" Mindy asked.

"Otherwise you'll have to stay with Mary Anne. You must have the proper equipment, or you'll freeze to death."

Mindy was stunned, but she understood.

"God will come through," Jeff said, pulling out a piece of paper. "Emil, could you go over our list of supplies?"

"Yes, but we'll have to hurry. I need to talk with Mary Anne and fix that door and get someone to stay with her. I must make sure she will be safe."

Warren called the airline while K.J. checked his camera equipment.

Emil scanned Jeff's list: heavy underwear, thick socks, liners, non-wrinkling walking shirts, thermal underwear, trekking pants, down or fiber-fill jackets, trekking books, insoles, moleskin, hats, gloves, money belt or pouch, water disinfection tablets, down sleeping bag, earplugs, bar of soap, water bottle, tissue, towels, notebook and paper, Bible, sweaters, headband, flashlight, medicine, and food snacks for energy.

"Looks pretty complete," Emil said. "I'm impressed."

Jeff folded it up and put it in his pocket.

"If I had my stuff," Mindy sighed, "it would really be complete."

❖❖❖❖❖❖❖

Waiting nervously for the doors of the government office to open, Jeff studied the ordinary, gray stone building. It reminded him of the drab government offices in Los Angeles. Inside, officials in brown uniforms prepared for the office to open.

"Nima is waiting for a call from us at home," Emil said to Mindy. "I think you two will get along. She seems shy, but that's only because she is struggling with so much."

"I'd like to get to know her," Mindy smiled.

Emil glanced at the office doors. "She would like that."

Jeff shifted his weight nervously from foot to foot. "It'll take a miracle to get these permits."

"Let's hope for the best." Warren looked up and down the street. "I need to find a pay phone. I want to give the airline a final call."

"Were you able to borrow any hiking gear?" Mindy asked.

Emil shook his head. "I found a few things, but nothing very good, I'm afraid. The boots are too big. They could give you severe blisters."

"What will we do if we can't go?" Mindy asked Jeff.

"We'll just..." Jeff paused a second, "just have to stay here in Kathmandu and make the best of it."

K.J. put both hands up in protest. "I've worked too hard preparing for this trip. I'm going up that mountain if it kills me."

"That could happen if you go by yourself," Mindy said. "It's a very dangerous hike."

"What's going to happen to me?"

"You could be attacked by the Abominable Snowman."

"Nice one, Mindy," K.J. said, looking uncertain.

Mindy looked back toward the mountains. "The story of the Abominable Snowman started in Nepal. The people call him 'Yeti.'"

Jeff snickered to himself as Mindy tried to look serious. "He must be real if he has a real name."

K.J. laughed nervously.

Mindy raised her eyebrows. "Everybody has heard of him. Years ago, someone discovered giant oval-shaped footprints in the mountains. They were more than a foot long and very wide. He even has a distinctive protruding big toe. Someone followed his footprints along a trail."

K.J.'s face expressed a mixture of worry and doubt. "If he isn't real, then where did you get all that information about him?"

Jeff and Mindy slapped hands together in glee.

"Don't want to go alone anymore, do you?" Mindy said.

Jeff finally laughed out loud.

Just then, the front door of the office swung open. Emil and Jeff rushed straight for the permit counter while the others waited outside. Trying to be calm, Jeff listened as Emil explained the situation in Nepali.

Seconds later, a big smile broke across Emil's face. Jeff was filled with hope as the official handed Emil a stack of papers.

Emil shook the agent's hand and turned to Jeff. "Let's go."

"Did we get them?" Jeff asked as they stepped outside.

Emil didn't answer as he studied the documents.

"Are we going?" K.J. asked.

Emil put his right thumb up. "These trekking permits were issued thirty minutes before the doors opened."

Jeff couldn't believe his ears. Chills raced through his body. Mindy stood with her mouth wide open.

"Where's Warren?" Jeff asked. "I've got to tell him." Looking around, he spotted Warren a block away talking on a pay phone. Unable to contain his new joy, Jeff ran toward him as fast as he could. Landing with a big jump, he beamed. "We got them," he cried. "We got them."

Warren had just put down the receiver. "That's great. I've got even greater news! The airline found Mindy's bag. We can pick it up on the way home."

Jeff's heart leapt. He realized again that God's timing was perfect. Wiping tears from his eyes, he yelled out the news to the others. Hearing about the found baggage, the team danced with excitement toward Emil's van.

"Does this mean we all get to go?" Mindy asked as she jumped in.

Emil started the van and grinned. "Let's hurry and pick up your bag. Then we'll get Nima. We could miss the eight-hour bus ride from Kathmandu to Pokhara if we waste too much time."

"Why can't we fly?" K.J. asked.

"We'll fly from Pokhara to Jomsom. Then we'll start the two-day trek up to Muktinath."

Tears escaped Mindy's eyes. She covered her face. "I'm really sorry," she said, looking through her hands. "Lately, my attitude has stunk. I didn't think there was any way we would get those permits today." She wiped her eyes, and her voice trembled. "This trip may be hard. But my heart is stirred over those kids. I can't rest until they're with Mary Anne."

Emil looked in the mirror at Mindy. "Remember, it's a long hike up that mountain."

The van roared along.

Emil glanced back at Mindy again. "I think you'll be good for Nima. She's only been with us for a year, and she has a lot of pain from her past. She could really use a good friend."

Jeff smiled, knowing that no matter what had caused Nima's pain, God would use his sister to help her heal.

It wasn't long before the team stood at the Kathmandu bus station and waited for the public bus to Pokhara. Jeff saw a bus that looked like a sheet-metal box on wheels. He hoped they would get a nicer bus than that one. Exhaust filled the air, making him cough, and the noise from roaring engines was irritating.

Mindy smiled at Nima and sat down next to her. Jeff winked at Mindy in approval. He knew that once his sister got focused nothing would stop her. Jeff smiled warmly at Nima, but she only looked away.

Warren walked up with a handful of bus tickets. "I'll keep these until the bus arrives."

"I wish it didn't take so long to get to Pokhara," K.J. sighed, rummaging through his backpack, which had been piled with everyone else's. "Are you sure we can't fly there?"

Emil pulled out his wallet and waved it. "I sure don't have the money to fly. Your budget is tight, too. Plus, think of all the footage you could shoot from the bus!"

K.J. zipped up his bag. "If it means getting some great shots, then I'm up for the adventure."

Emil looked at his watch. "It's nearly ten. Soon we'll depart. The bus driver allows lots of time to navigate the curves and steep hills, and he makes sudden stops and starts. If we stop and get off anywhere, you need to be extra alert. The driver gives little warning when he leaves."

"Why didn't we rent our own bus?" K.J. asked.

Jeff put his finger to his lips. "The budget, remember?"

"It'll be good for us to spend time with Nepalese people," Warren added.

The sudden loud roar of a bus engine startled Jeff. Hoping for an air-conditioned cruiser, he stared in dismay at the old yellow bus that rattled up. Mindy covered her mouth with a tissue to filter out some of the exhaust from the air. The bus horn honked twice.

"We should hurry," Emil said. "He won't wait."

The team piled into seats near the front. Nepalese men, women, and children climbed aboard wearing a mix of colors and styles. Mindy's eyes widened as people carried pigs, chickens, and other animals on board. Women dragged big baskets filled with goods to their seats.

To Jeff's surprise, two American trekkers greeted him as they passed by. They gave themselves away with their accent. As Jeff looked back, the two guys waved at him again.

More people filled the tiny seats and aisles. It was impossible for Jeff to stretch his legs.

"I feel like I just turned into a sardine," K.J. moaned, grasping his camera bag tightly.

"I'm going to smell like one," Mindy said.

Nima stifled a laugh.

Emil settled in. "I hope you're ready. We have eight hours of this."

Nima turned to Mindy. "The bus isn't even full. People will sit on the luggage racks."

Mindy's eyes grew wider. "You mean on top of the bus? Won't they fall off?"

A few seconds later, with a sudden jerk, the bus roared away. The pigs grunted and the chickens clucked. The bus screeched along, and soon, they were bumping along through the winding countryside. Jeff scanned the beautiful golden rice fields and high, contoured green terraces. He remembered from Mindy's research that the road followed three major rivers through fertile valleys. As they motored on, small towns and villages appeared, complete with bazaars, food stands, and shrines of worship. The bus jerked back and forth along the curves. Jeff tried to look over the edge of the dangerous cliffs along the way until, no longer able to fight sleep, he nodded off.

Later, Jeff's right eye popped open as the bus came to an abrupt stop. He felt groggy but was glad he had slept awhile. It was 1:30 p.m. He rubbed his weary eyes. "Why are we stopping?" he yawned.

"It's a potty stop," Emil explained. "A squatty-potty stop."

Mindy overheard and groaned in disgust. Her ponytail had come loose, and strands of her blond hair were sticking to her face. "We've used these toilets before in Asia," she said, trying to fix her hair. "A hole in the ground."

K.J. laughed. "I'm glad I don't have to go. But I'll see what kind of scenery I can film."

"It's only a matter of time," Mindy warned.

Emil stood up. "Remember, the driver will take off with or without you."

Everyone nodded and headed off the bus. Twenty minutes sailed by fast as the team stretched their legs and used the bathroom.

The bus was filling up when Warren climbed back on and checked for the rest of the team. "Where's K.J.?" he asked.

Mindy shrugged her shoulders.

A few more people piled on, and the driver shut the door. With a great puff of black exhaust, the bus roared off.

Without K.J.

Chapter 3

Terror in the Air

Jeff felt numb. "What do we do now?"

Mindy groaned. "I knew something like this would happen. He has to film everything in sight."

Warren and Emil struggled out of their seats. Navigating through the sea of bodies, they squeezed their way up to the bus driver. Jeff looked back, but the bus had traveled so far down the road that he could no longer see the potty stop. As Emil spoke, the driver shook his head. Again and again, he seemed to be refusing to turn around. Jeff felt like screaming, yet he knew frustration wouldn't solve anything.

Warren fought his way back. By now, all the people on the bus were staring at the team.

"Isn't he going to turn around?" Jeff asked.

"No," Warren said. "Not unless we pay."

"How much does he want?" Mindy asked.

"Ten dollars."

"K.J.'s not worth it," Mindy argued. "He better not keep us from getting those kids in time."

Without hesitation, Jeff took some bills from the team money pouch and handed them to Warren. After the driver grabbed them, the bus came to a screeching halt. The quick U-turn on the narrow road made everyone nervous. Embarrassed, Jeff kept his head down. Seeing the angry faces of the other passengers made him want to disappear.

K.J. looked up with relief as the noisy, smoky bus pulled up in front of him at the potty stop. His face was red with embarrassment as he stood up and dusted himself off. Avoiding the annoyed glares of the other passengers, K.J. quickly boarded the bus and made his way to the spot that Jeff had saved. After he squeezed in, the bus took off and roared once again up the mountain. Jeff snuck another glimpse at the sea of angry faces. Even the Americans looked annoyed. Trying to control his own anger, Jeff put his head down and closed his eyes.

Finally, K.J. broke the silence. "I'm sorry. I was filming some incredible mountain scenery, and then I realized that I should probably use the bathroom. I didn't know the driver would take off so quickly."

Jeff took a deep breath, trying to control his response. After a long pause, he shot a sober glance toward K.J. "Get your act together. Emil clearly warned us about this. It took lots of money and persuasion to get you back, not to mention that everyone else on the bus is mad at us now."

Mindy turned to K.J. with fiery eyes. "We didn't get our money's worth. I'm so angry at you. Try to remember—this trip isn't about a video. These kids' lives are at stake."

K.J. glared at Mindy as he slid down against the seat. Nobody would speak to anybody else, and the team soon fell asleep in the heavy silence.

The team slept hard until everyone on the bus was awakened by a strange thumping noise. The thumps got louder, and the bus began to shake wildly as the driver pulled over near a rest stop in a small town. Jeff glanced at his watch; it was six p.m. They had been asleep for some time.

"What's going on?" Mindy asked.

"I don't know," Jeff said. "There's obviously something wrong with the bus." Listening to the buzz of conversation, he wished he could understand the language.

"Now I really wish we could have hired our own bus," said a tired and embarrassed K.J.

Everyone watched and waited, until the driver ordered everyone to get off.

Emil talked briefly with the bus driver and then gave the report. "The bus blew a tire and broke the axle. There's nothing we can do. Hopefully, we'll still get to the hotel in Pokhara in time to get a little sleep tonight."

"We'll be okay," Mindy said. "We have a clear mission."

K.J., still feeling spiteful and not very optimistic, rolled his eyes at her.

Emil gathered the team together. "The driver says it will be at least an hour before another bus can get here. There's a food stand nearby. We can get something to eat or drink."

The team followed Emil to the busy plywood and metal outdoor stand. Stocked with food and drinks, it was a welcome sight. As the grill sizzled and the spicy aroma of cooking food filled the air, the line of hungry people got longer.

Looking behind them, Emil pointed up to a huge mountain range. "That's where we're headed. It's the Annapurna mountain range, part of the Himalayas."

Jeff's tired eyes tried to take in the beautiful scene. Up ahead, he saw contoured green terraces across the valley. He took a deep breath and knew the air was fresher. His eyes focused better on the scene above. Soon he was in awe of the majestic white-capped mountains.

Mindy pulled out a small notebook. "Let me tell you a little of what I learned about these incredible mountains. The Himalayas have six major summits, and all of them are over twenty-four thousand feet. They produce snow and glaciers that become huge storage systems of ice and water. When melted, they supply water for crops downstream to the dry places. That's why Annapurna means 'food giver.'"

"I'm impressed," Emil said. "She's a pretty thorough researcher."

K.J. found himself agreeing with him. "She knows her stuff," he added.

Mindy didn't need much encouragement to go on. "Close to a billion people in the world believe these mountains are sacred. There is no other mountain range on earth that figures so greatly in the religious beliefs of such a large and diverse population."

Jeff still couldn't believe what he was seeing and hearing. He was so glad to be there. Mindy turned the page.

"These mountains are considered the dwelling place of saints and even gods. The higher the mountain, the higher the god. Some think these mountains actually are the gods."

K.J. couldn't stop looking at the mountains and imagining what they would look like on film. Everyone was now captivated by the sight.

Jeff noticed the Americans behind them out of the corner of his eye.

The taller man moved closer. "Aren't you guys a little young to be out here?"

Jeff's body stiffened. He thought the man must be joking.

Everyone turned around to see who had addressed them.

Jeff held out his hand. "We're part of a club. My name is Jeff Caldwell, and we're working on a video project. What are your names?"

The tall man nodded slightly. His friend moved closer. With brown hair and full beards, both were dressed in ragged blue jeans, old jackets, and well-worn shoes. They had well-built, sun-tanned bodies.

"I'm Jay," the man said. "This is my brother Shawn. We're from New Jersey."

Jeff nodded. "I could tell by your accent that you were from that part of the country."

They laughed as Jeff introduced the others. Mindy put her book away and joined Jeff in explaining the club.

Shawn looked at Jeff with piercing dark brown eyes. "We've trekked this mountain many times and know how dangerous things can get. Try to keep an eye on your friend. You guys could get killed if everyone is not alert."

Jeff felt the strong warning in the words and thanked the brothers for the advice. Clearly, they were talking about K.J.

Finally arriving at the front of the line, Jeff bought a few sodas and some bags of chips for the team. They gathered around an outdoor table.

"I don't think those guys liked me," K.J. said.

Jeff turned toward his friend. "I think they gave us some good advice. Not everybody was happy about turning around to go back for you."

Mindy stood defiantly. "Maybe an apology to the whole bus would be in order after what you did."

"Look," K.J. said, his eyes almost teary. "I'm sorry. I'm glad you're so perfect and have never made a mistake."

"All right, you guys," Warren said. "Let's talk about this. We won't be effective as a team if we can't forgive one another and get along."

"Well, if our goal is to rescue these kids, we won't be very effective if we can't get to them!" Mindy retorted.

"Yeah, but we're a media club," K.J. said, glaring at his best friend's sister. "And we can't be a media club if we don't have any footage. I'm the one who is supposed to film it. I was just doing my job."

Warren broke the tension. "You're both right. We do have two objectives, and sometimes they might conflict. We'll have to compromise. K.J., you were warned that the bus could leave, and you should have been paying attention. Stay on your toes; in a place like this, slacking off could be dangerous."

K.J. smiled sheepishly. "I see what you mean. I was sure glad to see the bus coming back."

Mindy couldn't help laughing.

"And Mindy," Warren resumed, "staying angry will only create more problems. K.J. has already apologized, and there's no need to make him feel worse than he already does. Let's learn from our mistakes—it will make us a better team."

Mindy nodded. She and K.J. exchanged civil glances, but they weren't ready to talk to each other yet. K.J. explored some of the scenery while Mindy sat down next to her brother.

"Are you mad?" she asked him.

Jeff shrugged. "It kind of hurt my feelings when you said that K.J. wasn't worth ten dollars. I know you two don't get along sometimes, but he's my best friend and I care about him."

"I'm sorry," Mindy sighed. "I was upset, and I was harder on him than I should have been. He really gets us some great shots, but I'm worried about not getting to the kids in time."

"Your love for those kids is amazing, Mindy. But I don't think we can communicate God's love to the Nepalese people if we can't even love the other members of our team. That's all."

Mindy removed her glasses and wiped off the smudges with her shirtsleeve. "You're right, Jeff. It doesn't make any sense for us to show God's love and concern for the people of this country if we can't show it to our own team." She got up from the bench. "I'll go apologize to K.J."

After a little while, when Mindy and K.J. had joined them, Jeff turned to Emil. He had been waiting for the right moment to find out more about his family. Jeff felt now might be a good time. "Emil," he said softly, "I'm really sorry about what happened to your children."

Emil's expression became serious and thoughtful. Jeff wondered if he had made a mistake. Nima slowly turned away, and Warren looked a little nervous.

"I'm sorry," Jeff said quickly. "My heart went out to your wife yesterday. I just wonder..." he stopped.

"It's okay," Emil said, blinking away tears.

Everyone waited, listening intently.

Emil wiped his eyes and took Nima's hand. "After Mary Anne and I got married, we dreamed of having a large family." He paused for a moment. "I'm sorry. I didn't plan on this."

"You don't have to talk about it," Warren said.

"This is my fault," Jeff said. "I'm sorry."

Emil shook his head. "It's okay. I need to tell you this." He wiped away tears. "Anyway, our dreams came true after our two children were born. God had answered our prayers."

The teamed listened with an intense sympathy.

"Then a horrible accident took place. Our whole family was in a rickshaw. You must have seen those little carts on your travels before."

Emil paused a moment to wipe his eyes again. "We were having a wonderful family time on a clear Saturday afternoon when a speeding truck came out of nowhere. It changed our lives forever."

Jeff's heart broke as he listened.

"The big truck lost control and smashed sideways into the cart. It's a miracle any of us lived. My arms and legs were broken. Mary Anne had severe internal injuries, and the doctor didn't give her any hope."

Emil's lips quivered. "Our son died instantly." He paused. "Our daughter died the next morning. My whole world fell apart. I was really mad at God."

"How did Mary Anne survive?" Mindy asked, wiping her eyes.

"With the Lord's help, she pulled through. But she can't have kids anymore. We were devastated and heartbroken."

Deep feelings of anger and pain arose in Jeff's heart. Mindy wondered what Nima was thinking and squeezed her hand more tightly. No one moved.

Emil took out a handkerchief and blew his nose. "I'm sorry. I didn't know I'd be sharing this." A few seconds later, he smiled through his tears. "Something really good did come out of it. When we faced the reality that we could never have more kids, we realized we had too much love to keep to ourselves."

Emil gently put his arm around Nima. "A couple years later, we decided to adopt. That's when we found Nima. She's a gift from God."

Emil kissed his daughter. She smiled as he went on. "We love her so much. After a while, God spoke to us about adopting more kids. That's when we found out about Tenzing and Chandra. Can you see how much this means to Mary Anne?"

Everyone nodded. Jeff's heart was full of a new understanding and desire to help his Nepalese host.

"We want to open our home to many other kids in the near future," Emil said. "We might even start other homes. Even though our kids aren't with us, God used the accident to open our hearts." He wiped his eyes. "Our kids are with Jesus."

Mindy looked at Nima."How do you feel about brothers and sisters?" she asked.

Nima shrugged.

Emil gave her another kiss. Then he hugged her. "Nima is worried we won't love her anymore. But she has nothing to worry about. We have lots of love."

Nima looked embarrassed. Mindy gave her a hug, and Jeff realized how special the moment had been. Until the loud horn interrupted it.

"I think the driver is calling us," Emil said, standing up.

Warren got up and gave their host a hug. "Don't worry," he said. "No matter what, the Lord will help us rescue Tenzing and Chandra."

The driver's report wasn't good. Another bus wouldn't arrive for two more hours, meaning the team wouldn't get much sleep when the new bus finally got them to Pokhara. Early the next morning, from that city surrounded by lakes, they would fly, then trek, to a skyline dominated by the Annapurna mountain range and the perfectly shaped peak of Macchapuchare.

❖❖❖❖❖❖❖

Early Tuesday morning, the small tour bus provided by the hotel pulled into the Pokhara airport. The team hadn't arrived in Pokhara until midnight, and they were grateful for a few hours of sleep. Once off the bus, they moved into the small airport lounge to check in.

Jeff felt a new excitement. "How long will the flight take?" he asked.

Emil answered. "Forty-five minutes. Our biggest challenge is getting the first flight to Jomsom."

"Why's that?" Mindy asked.

Nima explained. "There is a lot of fog and wind near Jomsom. They may not let us take off."

Jeff listened as Nima spoke. She sounded relieved at the possibility that they might not go.

"We must catch that flight," Emil said. "After the fog lifts, the wind comes up. Jomsom is 9,300 feet high. That can create real problems."

"We have to make it," Mindy said. "This slow pace is driving me nuts."

"I don't think we need to hurry," Nima said. "The family is always making empty threats."

"That break-in yesterday wasn't too empty," Mindy countered.

Jeff looked across the tiny airport lounge. Shawn and Jay, the American trekkers, were coming through the doorway.

Jay walked up to them, a big smile on his face. "Hey, kids. Not much sleep last night."

Shawn laughed out loud, looking at K.J. "Sure was a wild bus ride."

K.J. crinkled his brow, and Jeff laughed.

Emil and Warren talked to the clerk at the check-in counter while Mindy and Nima sat on the pile of backpacks near the counter.

"It doesn't look very good," Warren said.

"What's wrong now?" K.J. asked.

"Jomsom has thick fog. The agent doesn't feel it's safe to fly a plane. They're going to wait as long as it takes for it to clear up."

"How long do you think that will be?" Jeff asked.

"It could be all day. Sometimes it is."

"Aren't we supposed to start our trek immediately after we land in Jomsom?"

Emil nodded. "After we land, we must hike from Jomsom to Kagbeni. It's a tough ten-mile hike up a mile-wide riverbed."

"What if we get in late? Can we hike after dark?"

"No," Emil said, looking at his watch. "We must get to Jomsom in the next couple of hours to stay on schedule."

"If we don't get there soon, that uncle will run off with the children," Mindy said. "I just know it."

Jeff remembered a Bible verse he had read in his devotions. "Yesterday I read a verse that said that God would make a way where there is no way."

Warren snapped his finger. "I read a verse about God opening doors that no man could shut."

Jeff smiled. "We need to share more often! But how can we go without a plane?"

The team waited impatiently for fifty long minutes. Finally, Emil went back to the check-in counter to see what was going on.

"It's getting worse," Emil reported. "Really bad."

"What's getting worse?" Jeff asked.

"The fog isn't lifting. Hopefully the wind will drive it out."

"We've got to go," Mindy said firmly.

"We have one other option," Emil said, studying a brochure. "We can hire a helicopter. It's the only type of aircraft that can land in this weather. But I'm not sure even they'll fly today."

"Let's try," Jeff said. "Maybe this is the door."

K.J. was enthusiastic. "I've always wanted to get footage from a helicopter."

"Come with me to the Everest Air counter," Emil said to Warren. "Let's see if they will fly their helicopter."

Jeff was nervous but trusted that Warren wouldn't allow them to do something crazy. In a few minutes, Emil and Warren hurried back.

"Looks like we're going to fly," Warren said. "Of course, we blew the budget by giving them some extra money."

"Will we be safe?" Jeff asked.

Warren nodded. "The pilot assured us that he'll turn around if it gets bad."

"Is there any other place to land except Jomsom?" K.J. asked.

"No," Emil said. "Jomsom is surrounded by peaks twenty-four thousand feet high. It's Jomsom or nothing."

"What do you mean?" Mindy asked.

"I mean it's land in Jomsom or return to Pokhara."

Shawn and Jay, who had been listening to the team's dilemma, walked up to Warren. "I wouldn't fly on that thing," Shawn said. "Be careful. Those Everest Air pilots are only after your money."

Everyone looked surprised.

"We've done this a few times," Shawn reminded them. "You'll never catch us on those choppers. We've seen a crash or two."

"We've got a deadline to meet," Warren said. "Emil feels it's okay."

"Emil has a good reputation as a guide," Jay acknowledged. "But we don't want to carry your bodies off the mountain."

"Thanks for your concern," Warren said graciously. "But I think we'll be okay. The pilot has promised to turn back if he has any doubt."

After saying good-bye to the brothers, the team headed to the chopper, which wasn't exactly what Jeff had expected. The old green military helicopter was big enough to hold twenty people. As he got in, Jeff felt the rush of air from the churning blades. Strewn about the body of the chopper were piles of boxes. He noticed the bench lining the belly of the cab and realized it was their seat.

As other trekkers got on, Jeff felt better. "It must be safe," he said. "These other people aren't crazy."

The door shut. As the chopper gained altitude, the roar of the spinning blades became deafening.

K.J. screamed at Emil. "Is it okay to take pictures?"

Emil nodded yes and pointed to a window. A gush of cold air filled the cabin, and they seemed to float higher and higher. Looking outside, Jeff saw the massive and icy Himalayas that K.J. was busy filming.

Jeff shouted to Emil. "How high will we go?"

"About nineteen thousand feet."

Jeff could feel the temperature rapidly drop as the chopper rose.

The team was freezing by the time the chopper, hovering high in the air, approached the Jomsom airstrip. Jeff prayed fervently. He tried to look down through the thick fog blanket, but Jomsom was nowhere in sight.

"How can the pilot do this?" Mindy wondered.

The helicopter hovered for what seemed a lifetime. Even if the team could have understood the words, the communication from the radio was filled with static. Out above the fog blanket, the huge mountain ranges surrounded them. Pushing away the frightening and nagging thought of crashing, Jeff wrestled with overwhelming fear. Then he noticed it. Smoke was pouring out from the engine compartment. It was filling the cabin.

"Oh no," Jeff cried.

They all tried to cover their mouth and nose with their clothes. Panic filled the cabin.

"What's happening?" Mindy screamed.

"We're on fire!" K.J. shouted.

Chapter 4

Twisted Ankle

Maybe those New Jersey guys were right," Mindy shouted over the noise. "We should have listened."

"Could be," Warren said, straining to see Mindy. "But their advice won't help us now."

"That doesn't look like smoke," Jeff cried.

Emil wobbled as he stood to his feet. "It looks like steam."

Jeff tried to stand, but the chopper was too unstable and he quickly fell. Finally, he was able to get up and look. "I think you're right. It is steam."

Mindy looked worried. "Is steam a good thing?"

"I don't think so," Warren said. "The engine is heating up. We've been hovering too long."

"I hope he can get this thing back to Pokhara," K.J. yelled. "My equipment is worth a lot of money."

Emil looked grim. "I don't think he's going back to Pokhara. He's got to land it."

Jeff remembered Emil's words about Jomsom or nothing. Jomsom didn't seem very safe at the moment. He sent up a prayer.

Finally, Jeff dared to look down again. A tiny opening appeared in the thick fog blanket. The pilot saw it and nosed the aircraft straight down. No one spoke until they saw a tiny airstrip next to a couple of old buildings.

"Is that Jomsom?" K.J. asked with surprise. "There's nothing there."

Emil leaned over to get a better look. "That's Jomsom all right. It's a little airstrip and a trekking lodge in the middle of the Himalayas."

They were all nervous and afraid. By now, Mindy had closed her eyes. Jeff figured they were losing altitude too fast. A rushing pain and a hammering headache racked his skull. The steam grew thicker, pouring out of the engine like a volcano as the chopper fell. Then there was a sudden and hard thud.

"We're crashing," Mindy cried. "We're gonna die."

"I think we landed," Warren said, gasping for air.

Shouting out a cheer, the passengers waited for the door to open. Two men rushed the chopper with fire extinguishers, but when they realized that instead of smoke the chopper was filled with steam, they pried the door open and began to help people out. Nobody on the team except Nima and Emil could understand them.

"They're telling us to get away from the chopper," Nima explained.

More than willing to obey the command, the team waited for their turn to exit. After Jeff jumped to the ground, he caught Nima. Mindy jumped out next, fighting the howling winds. She looked as pale as a sheet.

"I think I have to throw up," Mindy said, holding her hands to her mouth. "I feel really sick."

"It's altitude sickness," Emil said. "I've had it before, and it's no fun. You vomit and experience diarrhea at the same time."

"On the way down, my head felt like it was going to explode," Jeff said.

"Mine, too," K.J. cried. "That was intense."

"I'm going behind that building," Mindy said. Racing as fast as she could, she disappeared behind the dumpy airport lounge.

"I'll make sure she's okay," Nima said and followed closely behind her.

Jeff tried to calm down by studying Jomsom. It looked like a deserted command post. After a few minutes, he went to find Mindy. He stared at his sister in disbelief. Mindy's face was bright red, and her eyes were completely bloodshot.

"Are you going to make it?" Jeff asked.

Mindy nodded, then put her head between her knees. "I don't understand why there are so many battles."

"I'm sorry, sis."

"It's okay," she said. "I don't care how hard it is. I want those kids."

Jeff looked at his sister with amazement. "You're a very brave person. I'm really proud of you."

"I don't see how you could be. I don't even smell good."

Jeff and Nima laughed, and together they helped Mindy up.

"We'll let you clean up a bit before we start climbing," Jeff said. "Emil says we must depart if we're going to make Kagbeni by dark."

"I'll make it, Jeff," Mindy muttered. "Just give me five minutes."

After Mindy had had a chance to rest, Emil spoke to the team. "God protected us. But we need to be careful when we start hiking. Each day will be different. Today, we'll battle rocks and boulders for ten miles up this dry riverbed. It's easy to twist your ankle, so be careful. We don't have time to carry anyone."

K.J. agreed. "I might be strong enough to carry you all, but I sure don't want to find out," he joked.

"How are you doing, Mindy?" Emil asked.

"I feel pretty weak, but I think I can make it."

Emil looked her over for a moment. "You've lost a lot of fluid. Altitude sickness wipes out your strength and causes nausea. One of us will have to carry her backpack, especially in these winds."

Warren immediately stepped forward. "I'm feeling fine. I'll be glad to do it."

"I'll try to carry it," Nima volunteered.

"Are you sure?" Warren asked. "It's pretty heavy."

"I'd like to try." Nima glanced shyly at Mindy and hoisted Mindy's pack onto her back. Mindy thanked her with a smile, touched by Nima's determination and generosity.

Jeff asked for God's protection, and then they started their trek up the mountain. Ahead was the dry riverbed and dramatic scenery of the mile-wide Kali Gandaki River. The riverbed was the same width as far as they could see. Boulders and rocks of every size lay close together. Hiking would be very difficult, as some rocks were too small to walk on yet big enough to create an obstacle course. Walking safely would require total concentration.

"This is nothing but a wasteland," Jeff said, already slipping over a rock. He steadied himself. "What happened to all the water?"

"It's gone for now," Emil explained. "Only during a major monsoon season does water fill this bed. The Kali Gandaki River is just a fast-moving stream that runs alongside all this."

Jeff heard the sounds of the water that snaked its way from the mountains to the valley. "That's cool. And look at those majestic mountains."

Mindy dodged a huge boulder in her path. "I'd like to, Jeff," she said, "but I'd fall flat on my face."

"Is it like this all the way to Muktinath?" K.J. asked.

"No," Emil answered as Nima giggled. "Once we get to Kagbeni, everything narrows. The trail will change, the winds will get stronger. It's a different challenge."

Jeff inhaled deeply and gazed upon the grandeur of the mountains. He felt overwhelming awe for the magnitude of the glorious snow-covered peaks.

"Look at the size of those mountains—it's like we're in another world," Jeff said. "I've never seen anything so big. They're almost out of proportion."

"We are in another world," Mindy declared. "Where else do you find peaks rising twenty-four thousand feet?"

"Good point, Mindy," Warren agreed.

Horses, yaks, and donkey trains loaded with supplies zigzagged in both directions on the mile-wide trail. Nepalese men, women, and children trekked alone and in groups. Using a rope or woven band fitted to their forehead, men and women carried baskets full of goods on their back. Almost everyone had strange red markings on his or her forehead. As the team hiked on, they were greeted with big smiles.

"Can you imagine carrying something that heavy using your head?" Jeff asked, observing how the people carried their heavy loads.

Mindy rubbed her forehead while dodging another rock. "Ouch. Just watching them makes me tired."

Emil grinned. "They've had years of practice."

More smiling people passed them. "You were right, Emil," Mindy said. "These people are very friendly. I'm not used to that in Los Angeles."

Jeff realized how poor the people here were. They wore ragged clothes and torn shoes, and many had skin infections. As cold as it was, most children lacked warm clothes, and their runny noses were obvious signs of health problems. They wore thin sandals or no shoes at all. Jeff sadly understood why most Nepalese people die at a young age.

K.J. was paying more attention to what his camera was filming than to where he was walking. Without warning, his foot twisted on a softball-sized rock, sending him to the ground. "Man," he said, jumping to his feet in embarrassment. "It's impossible to walk around here."

Mindy tried to hold back but finally burst out laughing. "Looks like you might be the one who needs carrying," she teased.

"Very funny," K.J. said, limping slightly. "You'll see. I won't be the only club member to fall down."

"Don't do that dance on the edge," Mindy said, doubled over. "It'll be hard to find another cameraman."

"All right, you guys, enough. Let's conserve our energy," Warren said, taking Mindy's backpack from Nima. "We've got a ways to go."

"It's so cold and windy," Mindy shivered.

"This is just the beginning," Emil said. "Wait till we get to Kagbeni. And Muktinath is colder still."

"I wish I could buy these kids new shoes," Mindy said.

Nima smiled in admiration. "You have such a big heart, Mindy," she said thoughtfully.

Jeff's steps got lighter as he saw how God was using Mindy to reach Nima.

"Will we get a place to stay tonight?" K.J. asked.

Emil looked at his watch. "If we get there by dark," he said. "Since we're between the peak seasons for trekking, we should be fine. Otherwise we would have to send another guide to run ahead and make reservations."

An old man spoke to Jeff along the trail. Jeff glanced quickly at Nima. "What is he saying?"

"Namestey," Nima said.

"What does that mean?" K.J. asked, still limping.

Nima smiled, her teeth gleaming in the sunlight. "It means, 'The god in me greets the god in you.'"

"Is it okay for us to say that?" Jeff asked.

"Yes," Emil said. "It's like saying hello in America."

The more people he saw, the more Jeff felt compassion for them. He wished he could spend time with all of them.

After a while, Emil stopped the team for a rest.

Jeff wiped sweat from his brow, grateful for a breather. Leaning against a rock, he stretched out his arms. "How are you feeling, Mindy?"

"Okay. The desire to get the kids is motivating me."

"Why don't you give us a briefing on Nepal?"

Mindy was happy to oblige. She was always ready to fulfill her researching job. Taking out her tiny notebook, she flipped through the pages. Stopping at a marked place, she read:

"Nepal has nineteen million people. It is the size and shape of Tennessee. Its latitude is the same as Florida."

Jeff nodded with interest. Mindy read further.

"Nepal is known as 'a root between two stones' because it is squeezed dangerously between Tibet and China, which creates political headaches. Famous for its mountain ranges and for Mount Everest, Nepal is a Hindu nation and the birthplace of Buddha."

"She's very good at what she does," Emil said.

Nima sat close to Mindy as she finished talking. After a short pause, the team went on. Trekking higher and higher, they zigzagged around scores of rocks strewn along the dry riverbed.

Jeff looked at his watch. It was four p.m.

"I'm getting a little tired," Mindy said.

Emil encouraged her with a big smile. "We'll find you a trekking lodge. It's too dangerous to hike in the dark. We need a good night's rest anyway."

As Jeff hopped over rocks, he marveled at the number of hardworking people trekking up and down the mountain. Shawn and Jay came into his mind. He wondered if they got a flight out of Pokhara.

"We should get to Kagbeni in an hour," Emil said, interrupting Jeff's thoughts. "We've made good time."

"That's good," K.J. said, stepping around a rock. "We had a ton of exercise preparing for this trip."

"You guys are in pretty good shape."

"Well," Mindy said, "the altitude sickness wasn't in the plan."

"Are you feeling any better yet?" Jeff asked.

"I've come this far," she said. "I must admit I'm looking forward to a good sleep in a warm room."

"I'm sorry," Emil said, "but the room won't be very warm."

Looking up the riverbed, Jeff searched the horizon for Kagbeni. Straining his eyes, all he could see were white snow-capped mountains rising higher and higher. He called out to Warren. "It's my turn to carry the backpack."

Just then, Warren's foot buckled. He went crashing hard to the ground.

Jeff ran over to him. "Are you okay?"

Lying in a fetal position, Warren moaned in pain. Rocking back and forth, he clenched his jaw while holding his right foot. "I think I sprained it pretty bad."

Jeff helped Warren pull off his boot. From the agonizing look on his leader's face, Jeff could tell the injury was bad. They got the sock off, and Jeff examined Warren's ankle. It was already swollen. Warren tried to get up, but after a struggle he collapsed to the ground again.

Writhing in agony.

Chapter 5

An Angry Priest

Jeff stared at Warren in disbelief. "How can I help?"

Everyone huddled around the club leader. "Let's pray for his ankle," Mindy said. "We're in the biggest battle of our lives for these kids."

Everyone nodded in agreement. Jeff gently put his hands on Warren's ankle, and the others joined in prayer. After a passionate plea to the Lord, everyone waited to see if Warren could stand.

"Let me try." Warren gritted his teeth, slowly rising to stand on his feet, his weight on his good leg.

Everyone cheered.

Warren hopped a few feet. "It hurts, but I think I can walk. It might get stiff if I rest. Let's try to make it to Kagbeni."

As they walked, Jeff continued to pray, worried that his leader might not be able to make the hike.

Warren slowly limped along in the howling wind.

"Maybe I can get him a donkey train," Emil said. "We've got to get to Kagbeni."

They struggled on foot until a man leading a donkey train passed by and stopped abruptly in front of them. Emil spoke to the Nepalese man while everyone else wondered what was going on.

Finally, Emil walked back to Warren. "He's offered to give you a ride on one of the donkeys."

"That's great," Jeff said. "How much should we pay?"

"I'm working that out," Emil said. "It won't be much."

After negotiating with the man, Emil turned to Jeff. "He'll take him to Kagbeni for two hundred rupees. That's less than two dollars."

Smiling in agreement, Jeff paid the man. Emil helped Warren climb aboard the donkey.

"This man's an angel," Mindy said. "Or that donkey is."

Jeff caught a glimpse of Kagbeni. "That's a beautiful sight. I don't think I could go much farther."

"Me neither," K.J. limped.

Emil pointed straight ahead. "That area over there is called the Mustang—it's a restricted region; tourists have to get special permission to enter."

"Why is it restricted?" Mindy asked.

"Tibetan Buddhism is practiced there. Animals and even humans are sometimes sacrificed. Lots of tourists trek here, and the Tibetan Buddhists don't want the place to get a bad reputation."

Mindy's and K.J.'s eyes opened wider. Jeff stared ahead.

"We're only allowed to get near the edge," Emil continued. "Kagbeni sits right on the border of the Mustang."

"We should pause right here and pray for the Mustang region," Jeff suggested.

"Good idea," agreed Emil.

The group joined hands and prayed together that God would triumph over any powers of evil remaining in that region, and that the people there would receive the Good News of Jesus Christ.

They started again for Kagbeni, fighting the bone-chilling wind that tore at their bodies. Dust swirled around them, making it even harder for them to see. Jeff had to continually wipe grit from his eyes.

Finally, the exhausted team entered the town. The very narrow streets of Kagbeni were surrounded by large walls that kept the icy wind out. Similar to the walls, the houses were made of rugged stone and cinderblock. Old hotels and trekking lodges lined the street. Cows, chickens, and donkeys roamed in the road. Children played everywhere. Though it was cold, women washed their clothes in the icy stream that ran through town.

Jeff badly needed a drink of water, as everything was dry, dull, and dusty. Continuing to look around, he spotted a few shrines. The famous Hindu prayer flags were blowing wildly in the wind. Some of the tiny flags were shredded.

As the icy cold cut through his clothes, Jeff's legs throbbed with pain. He tried to imagine how Warren must be feeling.

Jeff pointed to the line of people ahead. "What's that?"

Emil wiped dust from his eyes. "It's a military checkpoint. We'll go through a number of them to get our trekking permits examined and signed."

Jeff nodded, wiping dust from his eyes as the team filed through the slow line.

Biting his lip in pain, Warren slid off the donkey and limped into the line. Emil finally got his permit signed by the man in uniform. When all the permits had been inspected, the team followed Emil.

Emil stopped in front of an old stone lodge with a flat roof. "I've been here before. It's four dollars per room."

Inside, Emil talked to the manager and paid for the two rooms. Jeff prepared himself for the worst. Candles lit the small rooms, while lanterns lit the larger areas. The rooms didn't have heat, electricity, or running water. Every drop of water had to be boiled or purified with iodine tablets before they could drink it. Jeff hoped he would be able to handle all this after the exhausting day.

Jeff, Mindy, and K.J. were stunned by what they saw inside the sleeping rooms. Flat bamboo mats were laid out on hard wooden frames. There were no mattresses; the team would be sleeping in sleeping bags on hard wood. Jeff could hear the icy wind howling through the gaping holes, as no two walls were perfectly square. But at least the tired trekkers could finally drop their backpacks.

The common dining area was the only place to get warm. A blanket was spread like a tablecloth over a large wooden dining table. Its edges hung well over the sides. Nima walked over to the table and lifted the blanket. Underneath the table was a coffee can filled with burning charcoal.

"So that's how you stay warm," Mindy said, shaking with cold. "I'll be spending a lot of time around that table."

Emil laughed. "You'll find them in most lodges."

"Some people crawl underneath the tablecloth to get warm," Nima said. "When we get to Muktinath, we'll all be under there."

"When do we eat?" K.J. asked. "That will warm us up."

"We should order the food," Emil said. "It'll take them at least an hour to cook it."

A tiny Nepalese girl greeted them as they sat around the table. She looked at them with large, placid eyes, and her nose ran slightly. Dressed in a torn brown dress, she looked very frail. After putting down a stack of dirty menus, she disappeared into a back room.

"I want to take her home," Mindy said. "She's the one who should be eating."

"You've got a beautiful heart, Mindy," Emil said with admiration.

"Thank you, Emil," Mindy responded. "God's given me a lot of love for kids."

"I'd like to love others as much as you do," Nima offered shyly. Nima was sitting next to Mindy again.

Jeff smiled at how the Lord was using Mindy's love to reach Nima's heart.

Warren rubbed his ankle as he listened proudly to his team members. He turned to Mindy. "You might want to sit under this blanket for a while. It's going to be a cold night."

Emil's and Nima's nods emphasized Warren's point.

Jeff put down his menu. "How's your ankle?" he asked Warren.

"It's better. After a good night's sleep, I'll be okay."

"I'm dreaming of a nice hot bath," Mindy said.

"Sorry," Emil smiled sympathetically. "You won't be bathing until you get to Tatopani."

"That's at least four or five days!" Mindy gasped.

"Without a bath," K.J. said, "we won't have to worry about the Abominable Snowman attacking you."

"Very funny," Mindy said. "You don't smell so good yourself."

"All right, you guys," Warren said. "Let's warm up with some hot tea."

By the time the team had ordered their food, the hot tea and hot coals had relieved some of the numbness in their limbs.

Jeff, however, couldn't get the Mustang region out of his mind. He looked to Emil for more information. "I'm confused about the Mustang region. You said they practice Buddhism in there, but I thought most Nepalese were Hindus."

Mindy pulled out her notebook. "Let me explain. I did some research on their religion. Many people in Nepal still worship lifeless idols and need Jesus."

Emil encouraged her to go on. "You're doing well. Please continue."

Mindy flipped pages in her notebook with new excitement. "Nepal is the only official Hindu country in the world. But that's pretty misleading because more than half of Nepal's population follow both Hindu and Buddhist teachings."

Emil nodded in approval.

Mindy read on. "In fact, I discovered that you should never ask Nepalese people whether they are Hindu or Buddhist. The people will always answer 'yes' because the two religions are so blended."

"But there is a difference, isn't there?" K.J. asked.

"I'll try to answer that. Emil will have to give the bigger picture."

Mindy turned another page. "Reincarnation is the central doctrine of Hinduism. Hindus believe that a good and dutiful life will earn a person rebirth into life at a higher level, again and again until he or she becomes one with the universe. But bad living can send a person backward in the cycle. It's the wheel of fortune."

"I've heard about that. They call it the circle of life," K.J. said. "Don't they have spiritual guides to get them on a faster path?"

"Yes," Mindy confirmed. "They believe that through good and compassionate living, a Hindu's spiritual growth will finally release him from the cycle of reincarnation. That's why they get up so early and carry ritual offerings to wake up their gods."

"Clearly explained, Mindy," Emil congratulated her.

"Thank God Christianity isn't about pleasing gods," Jeff said. "We don't have to earn our way.

Jesus did all that had to be done. We just have to accept it."

"Amen to that!" K.J. cheered. He studied the Nepalese people as they prepared the meal. A sudden desire rose up in his heart to help them find the one true God. "What confuses me is how many gods the Hindus worship."

Emil thought for a moment and then began to explain. "The highest god in Hinduism is Brahma. He is known as the creator. Vishnu is the preserver, and Shiva is the destroyer. Hinduism has millions of gods, including animals. Cows are especially sacred."

K.J. grinned. "What do they use for McDonald's?"

Emil laughed along with the others. "If you kill a cow, you can go to prison for life. Cows are not even used for plowing. Instead, men plow by hand."

"Why do all the people put that red stuff in the middle of their forehead?" Mindy asked.

"That's the way they associate with the gods. It's a paste made of grains and red powder that they offer daily to the gods, and then put some on themselves. Some have a little dot representing it."

"Wow," K.J. said. "That's devotion."

Warren nodded. "Now tell us about Buddhism, Mindy."

"Well, it's similar to Hinduism, and yet somewhat different. Buddha believed that things of this world are just passing illusions. He also believed that too much attachment to them causes pleasure and pain."

"He was right about that," Jeff said.

Mindy went on. "Buddha taught what he called the Middle Way of right living. By following his way, one could attain nirvana."

"And why would anyone want to attain nirvana?" K.J. asked. "What is it?"

"It's an end to suffering and a release from the cycle of rebirth, like in Hinduism. It's a state of eternal bliss."

"So both believe that you keep getting reborn as something else until you get off the cycle," Jeff said.

Mindy and Emil nodded in unison.

"That's why they blend so easily, yet are so different," Emil said. "You'll see signs of these beliefs everywhere. Monasteries, temples, prayer flags, and prayer wheels. They are all signs of religious devotion."

"What about Shangri-la?" K.J. said. "I've heard it's near the Himalayas."

Nima smiled.

Mindy laughed out loud. "Shangri-la is a myth about a happy kingdom hidden just beyond the Himalayas. It's where people are completely free from all the troubles of the outside world."

"Sounds good to me!" K.J. said with enthusiasm. "I vote that on our next trip the Reel Kids go to Shangri-la. What do you say, Warren?"

Warren laughed. "I suppose we could spread the gospel there, too!"

Everyone laughed in the midst of their exhaustion. Jeff, however, still couldn't get the Mustang off his mind.

"Can we visit the temple near the Mustang? I really feel that we need to pray for that area."

Emil stood up. "Let's go over there now while the food is being prepared."

Jeff jumped to his feet. "Anybody else coming?"

Mindy, Nima, and Warren shook their heads.

K.J. grabbed his camera and jumped up. "I'll go."

Moments later, the three were back outside fighting the wind.

"There it is," Emil pointed after walking a ways. "This Tibetan Buddhist temple is quite radical."

The sound of drumbeats grew louder as they neared the temple door. A large man with long, dark hair greeted them. He was cross-eyed and looked like he was in a trance. The man stared intently at Jeff and K.J., ignoring Emil. "One hundred rupees," he said in broken English, holding out his hand.

"The priest will let us in if we pay one hundred rupees," Emil said. "It's less than a dollar."

Jeff quickly got the money out.

"What do those drumbeats mean?" K.J. asked.

Before Emil could answer, the priest spoke. "It is the Lama."

"What is the Lama?" K.J. whispered. "This is kind of frightening."

"He's their high priest," Emil explained. "The Lama chants prayers with his drum."

Jeff handed the man some rupees. K.J. reached inside his jacket and clicked the camera on.

Emil quickly stopped K.J. from filming. "K.J.," he whispered, "you have to turn that off. It would be very disrespectful, not to mention against the rules, to take any kind of pictures in here. Maybe later you can film Jeff talking about what the inside was like."

The walls were covered with dusty, but once-colorful, tapestries. The smell of incense filled Jeff's nostrils. Ritual horns, drums, masks, prayer wheels, and statues of Buddha and the ancient Lamas were everywhere. Ancient books were stacked on shelves.

Hand-painted scrolls and sacred silver objects lay on dusty benches in dark corners.

The man who had greeted them began to nervously point to the door.

"He wants us to leave," Emil said. "He senses something is up."

Jeff looked at the priest and made a prayer gesture. Amazingly, the man smiled and nodded yes.

Knowing he had just a few seconds, Jeff began to pray. "Jesus," he prayed with his hands extended, "please break Satan's hold on this region so people will come to the true Light. Break the power of darkness over these two precious kids. Bring freedom to thousands by Your power."

With a sudden flare of anger, the priest began to shout at them and point toward the door.

"He's getting very angry. He realizes you're not praying to Buddha. We should leave."

"Look. I don't know exactly why," Jeff pleaded as they left, "but I feel we should circle the temple and pray."

"We should go counterclockwise," Emil said. "It's the opposite of how they do it."

The three quickly circled the temple. K.J. walked a few steps behind the others to film. They prayed with intense fervency until they realized that they were in trouble. The cross-eyed priest was screaming and running after them, and he held a Gurka knife in his hands. The man screamed even louder as he raised the knife in the air.

Chapter 6

Conflict at the Lodge

Feeling a sudden surge of fear, Jeff took a step back. "Do you see the look in his eyes?"

"He knows your prayers are powerful," Emil said. "He's yelling that the Lama is mad."

"How mad can a Lama get?" K.J. asked.

"I don't really want to find out," Emil said. "Nobody would ever know if he attacked us with that knife."

They ran as fast as they could toward the lodge.

Jeff decided to stop and look back. "Emil," he implored, "please be patient with me. I feel God has called me to stand at the Mustang region and pray for the kids. I need to be obedient."

Emil cautiously looked back and made sure the priest had returned to the temple. Then he pointed to a sign. "This sign is the edge."

"I want to pray there for just a moment."

"Okay," Emil said. "Just don't go beyond the sign."

Jeff extended his hands to pray. K.J. and Emil joined in and prayed for Tenzing and Chandra and the nation of Nepal. Then, looking toward the temple, they saw the priest walking their way.

"Does he know we're here?" K.J. asked.

Panic filled Jeff's heart. "Let's get out of here before he sees us again."

They sped toward the lodge and didn't look back. Once inside, an exhausted Jeff tried to catch his breath.

"What happened? Are you guys all right?" Warren asked.

"Just a run-in with an angry priest. We're okay," Jeff assured him, finally able to stand still.

Mindy was talking to the Nepalese woman who ran the lodge. Nima was interpreting for her.

Mindy turned toward Jeff with a look of joy on her face. "Let me introduce you to my brother, Jeff," she said to the woman.

Jeff sat down next to them and joined their conversation. Emil soon joined them, too. The food had not yet arrived as Mindy introduced them to her new friend.

"This is Dorjee. Her family runs the trekking lodge. We've been talking about spiritual things. She's interested in hearing about Jesus."

Jeff's heart filled with love for the short, dark-eyed woman with a red paste dot on her forehead.

Dorjee smiled at Emil and spoke to him in Nepali. Emil nodded, and Nima explained that Dorjee had asked if he believed in Jesus, too. Recognizing the woman's hunger for truth, Jeff prayed for her. In such a remote place, Dorjee had probably never heard the name of Jesus.

Jeff's thoughts were interrupted when the front door opened. His stomach turned. He hoped it wasn't the man from the temple. It was a relief and a surprise to see Shawn and Jay come through the door. He was almost happy to see them.

Jeff warmly greeted the exhausted-looking brothers. "Boy. You look pretty tired."

Shawn nodded as Jay strolled over to the table and sat down. "You guys survived the helicopter ride," he said.

Jeff nodded. "You were right, though," he said. "I thought we were going to crash." Then he turned to Dorjee. "Let me introduce you to a new friend. Her family runs the trekking lodge."

After exchanging greetings with Dorjee, Jay looked around for a menu. "We're kind of hungry. Can we get some dinner?"

Dorjee rose and brought him a menu as Shawn sat down to join them. Jeff wanted to continue telling Dorjee about the Lord and wondered how Jay and Shawn would respond.

"When did you guys get a flight?" Jeff asked.

"About noon," Jay said. "The fog finally cleared up."

After a few moments of silence, Shawn called out to K.J. "How is our mountain climber doing?"

K.J. looked up from fiddling with his camcorder. "Okay, I guess," he replied.

Jay pointed to something on the menu, and Dorjee retreated to the kitchen.

"The food isn't very good here," Jay said. "There's no way to get meat. Only a few things can grow up here, and the rest has to be trekked up the mountain."

Dorjee's daughter brought in a large tray of food. She put down each plate, then hurried back to the tiny kitchen to prepare more food. The plates were piled with a yellow curry sauce over a bed of rice, served with a few slices of carrot and potato.

"What is this made of?" Jeff asked curiously.

"Lentils and curry," Nima said. "It's a standard Nepalese meal."

Jeff took a bite and thought it tasted fine, but he could tell that K.J. wasn't as impressed. Jeff ate for a few minutes, but he couldn't get Dorjee off his mind. He wanted her to hear more about Jesus.

The group ate in silence until Shawn turned to Mindy.

"So what inspired kids like you to give up your Christmas vacation to make such a difficult trek?"

Mindy put down her spoon. "As my brother mentioned, we're part of a video club. Besides producing a video about Nepal, we're helping our guide adopt two children from Muktinath."

At first, Jeff was concerned that Mindy might say something that could put the kids in danger, but after more thought, he figured she would be okay. After all, their rescue mission probably wouldn't matter much to these guys.

"What inspired your trek?" K.J. asked the brothers.

Jay pulled his chair closer. "I've been on a spiritual journey for years. We've both been studying Buddhism and Hinduism. This is the place to get tuned in to who you are. Here you can learn to become one with the universe."

"Have you guys found everything you're searching for?" K.J. pried.

Shawn hesitated a moment. "We're looking for the path that will lead us to God. It takes time to find, I guess."

Jeff drew a deep breath. "Have you ever read the Bible?"

"No," Shawn replied. "It's just another book. Why should I take it seriously? I was raised in a Christian church, and I hated it. People were always telling me what I could and could not do."

Jeff prayed, not knowing how much he should say. He wondered where Shawn's bitterness came from and hoped it wouldn't prevent him from finding real truth in Christ. "The Bible makes things pretty simple. It states that Jesus is the only path to God."

"I've thought a lot about Christianity," Jay added. "I think that Jesus was a prophet."

"He's more than that," Jeff replied. "He's the Son of God who died to forgive us for all the times we've messed up. The only path to God is through Jesus. We don't have to earn acceptance from God. We just have to accept what Jesus has done."

Jay thoughtfully nodded his head but remained silent.

"You know," Shawn said, "I just hope you guys don't try to convert the people of Nepal. They know much more about God than any of us."

Jeff hesitated. He wanted to talk with them some more, but he also wanted to figure out a way to continue talking with Dorjee. He prayed quietly for a solution.

"If I were you," Shawn said, "I would get those kids from Muktinath and keep everything else cool. You could get in real trouble messing around these temples."

Jeff felt the firm tone of his advice.

Shawn went on. "Word travels fast around here. We heard about how you guys upset the priest in the temple."

Jeff swallowed hard and wondered if visiting the temple had been a smart thing to do.

Chapter 7

Trek to the Holy City

The group lapsed into silence. After a few moments of thought, Jeff was struck with an idea. He finished his food and excused himself. Mindy and Nima headed to bed, exhausted.

After Emil, Warren, and K.J. had joined him in their room, Jeff presented his idea. His eyes sparkled. "I don't know whether those guys are ready for the gospel tonight. But I know Dorjee is."

Everyone nodded.

Jeff took a deep breath. "I've got a plan. If Emil talks to Dorjee in Nepali, Shawn and Jay won't be able to interfere."

Emil agreed. "That's a good idea."

"If Shawn and Jay feel like talking for a while before they go to bed, K.J. and I will share with them."

The plan worked perfectly. Emil continued to talk with Dorjee, answering her questions and sharing with her about God's forgiveness. Meanwhile, Shawn and Jay discussed their search for truth with Jeff and K.J., who in turn shared that Christianity was not about following rules, but about having a relationship with Christ. The long day finally came to an end as the tired trekkers all went to bed.

After a short sleep, the morning rays announced the arrival of Wednesday. Climbing fully dressed from their sleeping bags, the team prepared for the trek to Muktinath.

Enjoying his breakfast around the warm table, Jeff was disappointed not to see Jay and Shawn around.

"Every muscle in my body aches," Mindy said. "But I feel stronger today. I'm ready to get those kids."

Warren raised his eyebrows. "I wish I could say the same. My ankle isn't any better. I'll need a donkey ride today."

Jeff didn't want to hear those words. "God is going to heal you. We need you."

Emil was concerned. "Warren needs to rest his ankle today. He has to improve by the time we hit Jomsom on the way down. We'll be trekking back to Pokhara, not flying, and the trails there are too narrow and dangerous for a donkey train."

"I'll be fine by then," Warren assured them.

"How are you doing, K.J.?" Jeff asked.

"I'm on my toes," K.J. grinned. "Anything could happen on this trek."

"How did it go with our New Jersey guys?" Mindy asked.

"I really think they're on a sincere search for truth," Jeff said. "They just don't realize that Jesus is the Truth."

"But," K.J. asserted, "if they're searching, aren't they supposed to be open?"

"Easy, K.J.," Jeff said. "In their minds, they've already been open to Christianity and it didn't work. It seems like past experiences with the church have made them pretty bitter, especially Shawn."

"What happened with Dorjee?" Mindy asked, turning to Emil.

"Something to celebrate!" Emil exclaimed. "I spent over three hours with her. After discussing the life of Jesus, I carefully explained the salvation plan to her. She invited her husband and daughter to listen."

"That's great," Mindy said.

Emil beamed. "Dorjee accepted Jesus last night. Her husband and daughter were open but apparently not ready."

"We'll pray that Dorjee will lead them to Christ," Warren promised.

"This is so exciting," K.J. said. "We all had a little part in it. We'll pray for their family every day."

"I left them some literature, and I can visit them when I take people on treks," Emil added.

Jeff felt excited and frustrated at the same time. In a nation shrouded in darkness, God had opened a tiny door for the light. But Jeff wanted more.

❖❖❖❖❖❖❖

It was late afternoon as the team approached a small town.

"Is this Muktinath?" Mindy asked.

"No," Emil said. "We still have a ways to go. This is Zargot, a capital of the past. It's a small trading city. We won't get to Muktinath for two more hours."

Jeff looked straight up the mountain. He saw some tiny black dots way above them on the hillside. "That must be Muktinath," he guessed, pointing up.

"Yes. You have good eyes."

Jeff gathered his strength and made his way up. A skeleton-like man walked barefoot down the stony path toward them. He was wrinkled, dark-skinned, and very dirty. He wore a cloth hat over his scraggly hair and had a goatskin around his shoulders. Clad in a ragged loin cloth, he supported himself with a cane and carried a cloth bag. He looked wild and somber at the same time.

"Namestey," he said as he passed.

"Namestey," Jeff said back.

"He's returning from Muktinath," Emil explained. "He probably visited the temple of Jwala Mai. It's the second holiest shrine in Nepal. Muktinath means salvation. Just as a Muslim dreams of visiting Mecca, a Nepalese believes he can find salvation if he treks to Muktinath. That man might have just finished his dream journey."

Jeff pondered Emil's words, thankful for his insight.

Outside of Zargot, they spotted a small industrial center.

"What's that?" K.J. asked.

"It's a sausage factory. A rare find up here."

Jeff looked over the low wall. Workers butchered the animals, separated parts, cut up the livers, and stuffed and tied the long lengths of slippery gut.

K.J. quickly got his camcorder going, but the embarrassed women turned their heads away.

Emil explained the very strange scene. "These people are most likely part of a neglected butchering tribe. I'm sure they wouldn't be allowed to live within the walls of the town."

Mindy was curious. "Sometime you'll have to tell us about the caste system here. It seems so unfair."

"We'll talk about that later. First let's get to Muktinath."

Jeff noticed that the fields had already been harvested. "What grew there?"

"Potatoes and buckwheat," Emil said. "It was harvested a few weeks ago. You grow what you can in this altitude. Zargot used to be famous for its elegant palace, shrines, and a large monastery. It was a pretty large town." He pointed to the right. "Over there stand the crumbling ruins and a few run-down houses."

As they passed above Zargot, Jeff saw a red-robed monk. His head was shaven, and he wore bright blue sneakers. Resisting the urge to chuckle at the unusual combination, everyone managed to keep a straight face.

Jeff looked up and saw Muktinath on a shelf above some slumping glacial earth. He thought of the temple that was there. "Why is that temple so sacred?"

"It is sacred to both religions because fire and water came out of the same rock," Emil explained. "They think it was from God. In the back of the cave near the temple grounds, water bubbles up through the deep mountain rocks. On either side of the water course is a thin jet of natural gas. Hence fire and water."

"I'm getting a headache," Mindy said. "It can't be..."

"It's probably the high altitude."

"Am I going to get sick?"

Emil was reassuring. "Muktinath is 12,500 feet high. If we slow our pace, it should help."

Slowing a bit, the team continued up. Every step became more difficult to take. For a moment, Jeff envied Warren bouncing along on the tired, old donkey.

As they entered the city around seven p.m., the officials were checking everyone along the trail.

"Here we go again," Mindy said. "Another checkpoint."

Moving into the line of trekkers, horses, yaks, and donkey trains, Jeff got a better view of the town ahead. He knew Mindy couldn't wait to get her arms around the two kids. He just hoped they had made it in time.

Mindy suddenly let out a scream of shock and terror. Her whole body was jerked straight up into the air. "Hey," she yelped. "Put me down."

Jeff stared in disbelief. A big yak had poked its horns into his sister's backpack and was suspending her in midair.

"I'm going to kill this thing," Mindy yelled.

"You could go to jail. You know, like for killing a cow," K.J. said, entertained by the sight of Mindy balanced on the animal's horns.

Mindy screamed louder still, turning the heads of people on the trail. Jeff didn't know what to do.

"Get this stupid thing to let go," Mindy said, trying to shake loose.

"We'll get you down," Warren cried from the donkey.

Emil and the yak owner lifted Mindy and pulled her from the horns. The yak got even angrier, trying to kick everyone in sight.

"That hairy beast has an attitude," Mindy said. "I'm not getting near one of them for the rest of the trip. Let's hurry up and get those kids and get out of here."

As everyone chuckled, Mindy's face became fiery red. "I'm sick of the enemy hassling me. I'm angry."

"That was not the enemy," K.J. said. "It was a mad cow."

The team finally got to the front of the line. After moments of discussion, the agent herded the team to the side.

"What's wrong?" Jeff asked. "What's he saying?"

"They want to talk," Emil said. "They got a complaint from the Lama in Kagbeni. They're pretty upset."

"Here we go again," Mindy said. "You shouldn't have gone to that temple."

"I'm sorry, you guys," Jeff said. "But I still believe we needed to pray there. Something broke loose in the spirit there. That's why things are heating up."

Mindy looked around for other yaks. "Can we fast forward to the end of this story?"

Everyone waited impatiently as Emil talked to the agent. After a few moments, Emil motioned for the team to pass through. Jeff was anxious to know what happened.

"In Nepal," Emil explained, "Lamas have tremendous power. The agents were going to make us turn around. But I apologized for you. They said they understood that Americans aren't familiar with the culture. I promised to educate you."

Jeff was grateful for Emil's wisdom and quick thinking.

As they walked into Muktinath, where Tenzing and Chandra would be waiting, Emil took hold of Nima's hand and held it tightly. "I know you've been struggling with the idea of bringing these children into our family," he said. "Mary Anne and I love you very much, and we always will. You are special to us, and you will be special to these kids, too. Just think how wonderful it will be for them to be loved by a big sister like you."

Nima hesitated. "I'm still nervous, but I sure don't want those kids to get hurt."

Emil gave her a big hug. "I'm proud of you. Now let's go get your brother and sister and take them home."

Everyone was amazed at what they saw in Muktinath. It was much different than they had envisioned.

"Emil, why is this place so small?" K.J. asked.

"The higher you get, the smaller the town. Muktinath's population can't be more than a thousand."

Jeff estimated Muktinath to be the size of a small city block. One street lined with old stone buildings ran through the center of town. Since the town wasn't walled, Jeff could see the host of shrines and the two main temples above it. He also could feel the bone-chilling wind. Along the street were some trekking lodges, a small teahouse, and what looked like a police station. Policemen were sitting outside playing some kind of board game.

"Where does the grandmother live?" Mindy asked Emil. "Let's hurry."

"In one of these old buildings. Just a minute." After studying a piece of paper, Emil looked from side to side down the main street. "It should be over there," he said, pointing up the road.

Jeff knew they had to locate the grandmother soon. As the sun went down, darkness was beginning to blanket the city. The evening grew even colder, forcing everyone to zip their jackets up high. Water froze as it ran down the hill, and the ground became slippery with ice.

Emil came upon an old building and knocked at the door. Mindy stood right beside him. Jeff knew she couldn't wait any longer.

An older woman opened the door looking frail, gray, and tired. Her eyes were lively yet weary. As Jeff studied her, he remembered that most Nepalese people die in their thirties. He was witnessing a miracle.

As Emil spoke with the woman, she became distressed. Finally Emil turned to the team.

"The kids are gone."

Chapter 8

Search and Rescue

Mindy was crushed. "It's their uncle Goray, isn't it? Where did he take them?" Tears rushed down her flushed cheeks.

Nima was silent as everyone else expressed their dismay.

For the next few moments, Emil questioned the grandmother. Then he spoke to the team. "Goray may have taken them to a mountain hideout, but she believes he's still in Muktinath. He'll probably take them out another route. She's had the other uncles searching for them in Muktinath, but they haven't had any success."

"We have to look for them right now," Mindy said. "This town isn't that big."

"Hold on, Mindy," Emil said. "I want these kids more than anybody. But the grandmother and uncles are exhausted. She suggests we get some rest."

"They'll be gone if we wait till morning," Mindy protested.

Emil pulled his jacket tighter. "It's too cold to look now, and besides, we need the family's help. We'll meet the uncles at seven. They're ready to carry the kids down if we find them. Tonight, as always, we must leave Tenzing and Chandra in the Lord's care."

Mindy bit her lip and reluctantly followed the others to the trekking lodge. The winds gusted even stronger.

Jeff was freezing, and his breath looked like smoke as he exhaled. "Let's get out of this deadly air," he shivered.

The lodge was similar to the others. It had a common eating area complete with blanket and hot coals, and no running water or electricity. A locked glass cabinet was filled with candy and toiletries for sale. And there was a common bathroom with a squatty potty. But this lodge was much colder inside. Almost unbearably colder.

It was impossible to get warm. Mindy and Nima shivered as they nestled under the table, where the heat from the burning coals was hottest. Everyone chowed down on the curried lentils and rice.

"Today," Jeff said, "I had the chance to read my Bible when we stopped to rest. I found an awesome verse talking about the whole earth being filled with God's glory."

"That's great," Warren said, his mouth open wide for a big bite. "God is giving us a lot of understanding on this trip."

Jeff put his spoon down. He felt confused. "I don't get it. If God wants to fill the earth with His glory, then what happened to Nepal?"

"What we see in Nepal today is the result of centuries of a nation living without the light and truth of the gospel," Warren replied.

Jeff wiped his mouth. "Why haven't more Christians come to places like this? Americans hear the gospel continually. What about the people here? And those in India, Bhutan, and Tibet?"

"I'm glad Americans get to hear the gospel," Warren said. "But Christians need to spread the gospel to the people who haven't heard it before."

"Exactly," Jeff agreed. "Can you imagine the joy in Nepal if the glory of the Lord filled it?"

"That's why we share the gospel," Warren said. "We do it because we love God. We want to see His glory fill the earth. We want people to know of God's love and that His Son paid for our sin on the cross."

"What exactly is the glory of God?" K.J. asked.

"Remember in Exodus 34 when Moses asked God to show him His glory?" Warren asked. "God answered Moses by showing him His incredible goodness and character."

"That's right," Mindy said. "So God wants to fill Nepal with His goodness so that the people will be drawn back to a relationship with Him."

"Remember to pray for this before you go to sleep tonight," Warren urged them.

Everyone agreed, taking away a bigger dream of what God could do in Nepal.

The first streaks of a brilliant dawn lit up the next morning. Looking out through warped window frames, Jeff saw the beautiful Himalayan mountains. Instantly, he remembered the passage that proclaimed how the heavens declared the glory of God. His spirit soared as he took a deep breath of fresh air. Soon it would be Christmas, when millions would celebrate the birth of Jesus, whom Jeff knew the Bible called the radiance of God's glory! They would celebrate God's great love in sending His Son into the world to save it. Thinking of this, Jeff prayed that Tenzing and Chandra would be home with Mary Anne, Emil, and Nima in time for a special Christmas celebration. Today he and the team were consumed with one goal: They must find the kids.

At the grandmother's old stone house, the door opened before Emil finished knocking. Inside, Emil explained that Warren had stayed back to rest his ankle, and the grandmother introduced Emil, Nima, and the team to the two uncles. Emil translated. "This is Ang Fu and Passang. They will help with the search."

Looking at the husky, dark-skinned men, Jeff could see how rugged life in the high mountains was. The uncles' eyes were friendly, yet their faces were worn.

After a brief discussion, everyone was anxious to begin the search.

"How do we know Goray hasn't already sold the kids?" Jeff asked.

"We don't," Emil said. "But Ang Fu and Passang feel deeply that Goray is still in town. No one saw him leave. Ang Fu thinks one of his priest friends is hiding them in the temple area or in one of the shrines. If we find them, we will depart in a hurry and take a different route back. It's a much faster descent."

"What if we don't find them?" K.J. asked.

"We've got to find them," Nima said. "We can't let Goray sell them."

"You're right, Nima. We *will* find them," Mindy stressed, excited to see Nima's growing concern for Tenzing and Chandra.

"Let's try the temple first," Emil suggested.

The determined team members headed northeast out of town and hiked a quarter mile up the mountain. Jeff was nervous and impatient. Then he saw the Hindu temple, a large stone building surrounded by a host of little shrines with gothic-looking wooden doors. They hurried up the temple steps.

Emil paid a young girl to guide them. Inside the candlelit temple, everything was dark and dusty. Paintings, graying prayer flags, and gifts for the gods lined the walls. A few Hindus lay on the floor chanting lengthy prayers. Jeff realized again the deception of darkness. People weren't finding God, only emptiness.

Careful not to disturb those praying, the search party looked around the temple. It didn't take long to conclude that the children weren't there.

Moving outside, Jeff saw a number of poplar trees. Below them were one hundred and eight water spouts in the shape of boars' heads. Cleansing spring water poured out of each one.

"I don't think they're in this area," Mindy said.

"No," Emil agreed. "Neither do Ang Fu and Passang."

A priest walked up to Jeff to smear red paste on his forehead.

Stepping back in a hurry, Jeff put his hands up. "Tell them I don't want that on me."

Everyone backed away.

"Let's get out of here," Emil ordered.

Ang Fu and Passang led them from door to door, inquiring after Goray and the children. Mindy and K.J. stopped when they spotted two ragged, skinny kids standing alone behind a building.

"That must be them," Mindy said. "They sure look like the kids in the pictures Mary Anne showed us."

K.J. wasn't so sure. "Shouldn't we ask Ang Fu and Passang to take a look?"

"No." Mindy was firm. "Let's take them now. This could be our only chance."

K.J. shrugged his shoulders. He picked up the boy as Mindy carried the girl, and they ran up the street toward the rest of the group. Before Emil could get a good look at the kids, a woman came running down the street, screaming and waving her arms.

Emil reached for one of the children. "I think you took the wrong kids."

Mindy turned red with shock and embarrassment. The terrified woman ran up with two policemen, who had abandoned their board game as soon as they heard her screams. Frightened, Mindy and K.J. set down the kids, who immediately ran to their mother. After grabbing them, she stepped back and started yelling at the policemen.

Mindy started to cry. "It was a mistake. I didn't mean any harm."

The policemen headed for Mindy and K.J.

A horrified Mindy stepped back. "I'm so sorry!"

Emil quickly explained, apologizing profusely to the mother and to the policemen. The policemen left as the angry mother hurried off with her children.

"Maybe those policemen know where the kids are," Jeff said.

"I've asked. They don't know anything. But they invited us to contact them if we need to."

Mindy sighed. At that moment, Jeff looked down the road and saw Shawn and Jay headed their way.

"What's going on?" Shawn asked. "Did Emil get the kids?"

Jeff shook his head. "Not yet. But we're working on it."

"What were the police here for?" Jay asked. "And why was that woman so upset?"

"It was a mistake," K.J. said. "It's worked out now."

"I hope so! Keep out of trouble!" Jay admonished as the brothers walked away.

"Maybe we'll see you later," Shawn called back. "We're on our way to the temple."

Emil got the team focused. "It's almost ten," he said. "We need to find the kids soon to get them out of here today."

"Why don't we pray?" Mindy suggested. "God can lead us."

Everyone agreed and gathered together.

Jeff bowed his head. "Lord, we're at the end of our rope. Please help us."

Just then, Mindy's eyes brightened. "I saw a picture in my mind. It looked like those small shrines. The kids were trapped behind a big black door."

"There are some shrines right up the road," Emil said after explaining Mindy's vision to the uncles. "Let's go."

Climbing halfway to the temple, the team stopped at the first shrine. Emil took Nima's hand as he knocked at the door, and everyone waited with expectancy. A priest dressed in a white robe opened the door, then quickly closed it before Jeff could look inside. Emil kept knocking. Finally, the priest opened the door again. Jeff peered inside, and to his shock, a little girl and boy sat crying on the floor. The uncles got excited.

"It's Tenzing and Chandra!" Emil cried out with joy. He pulled out the adoption papers and spoke to the priest. Then he turned to the team. "The priest says he's a close friend of Goray. He will release the kids only to their grandmother no matter what papers I have. So I'm going to get her and bring her here."

The uncles sat inside with the children while the team waited outside, nervous and unsure. Standing near the shrine, they prayed.

"I knew God would help us," Mindy said.

Just then, Shawn and Jay came by on their way back from the temple.

"What's going on now?" Shawn asked.

"We've got the kids," Mindy said.

Jay recognized the children. "Hey, we know their uncle Goray. Does he know you're taking them?"

Jeff stepped forward. "Everything is fine. Emil has legal adoption papers. The kids' uncles are helping carry them down the mountain."

"Cool," Shawn said. "We'll be staying here a few days. Have a safe trip down."

"You guys be careful," K.J. said.

"You be careful, too," Jay said, walking away.

Soon the team saw Emil and the grandmother riding up in a rickshaw. Tears streamed down the grandmother's face as she got out of the cart. She went inside and kissed her grandchildren over and over.

"It must be very hard for her to give them up," Mindy said. "I can't imagine."

Finally the grandmother approached Emil. After hugging him, she looked him in the eye and spoke with tears streaming down her face.

"What's she saying?" Jeff asked.

Emil translated. "She says her heart is broken. She knows she will never see them again. But she knows this is the right thing to do. She says she will try to convince Goray."

After Ang Fu and Passang carried the kids out of the shrine, the grandmother hugged her grandchildren again. Finally, she handed them back to the uncles and began to weep even harder.

Hugging the frail woman, Nima spoke briefly and quietly to her. "I told her not to worry," she explained to the group. "I told her that we will take good care of them."

The priest comforted the distraught grandmother as the others headed back to the lodge.

Emil gathered everybody together. "We have to leave in fifteen minutes. Goray will be back at noon."

Jeff looked at his watch. They had one hour.

Chapter 9

Escape

Jeff hurried to get ready for the descent. Glancing at a map, he realized again what a grueling downhill hike it would be. It would take the rest of the day to get to Jomsom. Since the shortcut they were taking was a four-thousand-foot descent, it would be extremely tough on their leg muscles. Warren would have to catch another donkey train. Jeff took out some beef jerky, knowing he would need extra energy.

After packing his backpack, Jeff headed for the common dining area. Mindy and K.J. were there already, playing with the kids. Soon Nima, who had been watching from across the room, walked over and joined them.

"These kids are so cute," Mindy said.

Chandra looked frightened. She was three years old, though her frail body made her look much younger. With big eyes, a dirty, rounded face, and messy hair, she captured Mindy's heart. Five-year-old Tenzing was bigger, with the same facial features and a playful smile.

"Thank God for those donkey trains," Jeff said as Warren hobbled into the room.

"I need to make a decision soon," Warren said.

"What do you mean, a decision?"

"If my foot doesn't improve, I'll have to take the plane back to Pokhara and wait for you there."

"No way," Jeff said. "We can't make it without you."

"I can't jeopardize this trip anymore," Warren countered. "It's one thing to get the kids. It's another to get them down the mountain. I will be dead weight, and I'll hold you back."

"Why don't we all take the plane?" Mindy asked.

"For a number of reasons. One is that Emil can't afford to buy tickets for the uncles and the kids. Also, since we saved time by flying to Jomsom instead of trekking, we missed a good portion of the trek. But we can see it, and film it, if we trek down."

K.J. brightened. "You mean we'll get to film Marpha after all?"

"Right," Warren continued. "And remember, Tenzing and Chandra have never seen an airplane, or even a car. A flight would traumatize them."

"Things may get dangerous," Jeff said.

"You're in good hands," Warren assured them. "Emil really wants to show you Marpha. Almost none of the people there have ever heard the gospel."

After a word of prayer, Emil found a donkey train for Warren.

"We're going to be chased down this mountain," K.J. said, zipping up his bag. "I heard old uncle Goray is a pretty good trekker."

"Maybe," Mindy said, picking up Chandra. "But we're going to get these kids home to Mary Anne."

"I hope she's okay," Jeff said. "And I really hope we don't meet any other crazy relatives along the way."

Trekking down the mountainside wasn't as difficult as Jeff had thought.

"There's not a lot of exposure on this hike," Emil observed.

"What do you mean by 'exposure'?" K.J. asked.

"Exposed places are openings along the trail," Emil explained. "Like cliff edges that are close to the trail, or other places where a fall could be dangerous. We will encounter them after we leave Jomsom."

"I like this part of the trail," Mindy said. "That ridge provides some security."

Jeff observed how Passang and Ang Fu hiked down while holding the kids in pouches around their backs. Chandra cried for a while before going to sleep. Tenzing kept grinning at Mindy.

Nima hiked with Emil but joined Mindy every once in a while. Now that they had the kids, Mindy knew that Nima's battle with insecurity would become more intense.

Two hours later, Jeff saw Mindy wincing.

"My feet are on fire," she said when Jeff asked what was wrong.

Emil overheard. "I hope you're not getting blisters. If your feet slide around too much on this steep hike, it will create friction. We'll be sure to check them later."

Jeff noticed that this trail wasn't as busy as the trail through Zargot. He walked alongside Emil, hoping for a chance to talk. "What can you tell us about the Hindu caste system?" he asked.

Emil glanced behind them to locate the others. Mindy took a few quick steps so she could listen.

"The caste system is a Hindu belief that separates people into different classes," Emil explained. "Nepalese generally fall in one or two classifications: The first is Indo-Aryan. That's people from the Indian subcontinent of Asia. The second is Mongolian, people from northern and eastern Asia."

"I read all about that stuff," Mindy said, referring back to her research. "The categories are broken down more than that, aren't they?"

Emil guided the team around a steep turn, waiting for K.J. to catch up before continuing. "There are sixty-four castes. The system violates what Scripture says about all of us being made in the image of God. Hindus believe that the highest god is Brahma. The highest caste of people come from his head. Those are the Brahmans or priests. The next level comes from his body. These are the warriors. Then the traders and artisans come from his thigh, and the lowest class comes from his foot. They're the shoemakers, butchers, blacksmiths, and sweepers. They're the untouchables."

"How can people treat other people like that?" Jeff said. "Nobody is untouchable."

"In Hindu culture, some are. That's why you should never point your foot at anyone. It's very offensive to a Hindu."

"Very interesting." K.J. raised his eyebrows. "I wonder what class Mindy came from."

"From the fist," Mindy teased back, lightly punching K.J.

"So that is why Hindus want to lead a good life," K.J. said. "So they can be reincarnated to a higher level. I get it now."

"Good job, K.J.," Mindy said. "I think you just moved up a level. But if you keep teasing me, you're going to come back as a wild monkey in your next life."

"Very funny, Mindy."

Hiking along, Jeff's thoughts turned to Goray. He wondered how Goray would react when he realized the children were gone. And he wondered how close he might be to them. "Emil, what do you think Goray will do?"

"Ang Fu and Passang told me he's really dangerous after he's been drinking. They say he drinks a lot."

"I'm glad we didn't know that," Mindy said. "Until now."

"What will we do if he shows up?" Jeff asked. "Won't the adoption papers settle it?"

Emil wiped some sweat from his brow. "Remember, it's not final until January 15, and he's not above trying to steal them back."

"He won't do that," Mindy said. "Not from us."

"There isn't much we could do if he did," Emil said. "Our nation doesn't protect kids like it should. He could sell them easily."

"It's not going to happen," Mindy emphasized.

Jeff looked back at Warren bouncing along on the donkey. He wasn't too thrilled at the possibility that Warren might not stay with them.

❖❖❖❖❖❖❖

Much later, the trekkers had left the steep loop and were now moving along the dry bed of the Kali Gandaki River. They walked the trail strewn with rounded boulders.

"Watch out for the rocks," Emil cautioned. "We don't want someone else spraining an ankle."

"My feet are burning up," Mindy said. "I don't think there's any skin left."

"I'm sorry," Emil sympathized. "You might have some serious blisters."

"Will we be able to do anything about it?" Jeff asked.

"We'll check at the lodge. She'll have to bear the pain until then."

"She's pretty determined," Jeff said. "She'll make it." Just then he looked ahead and saw what appeared to be a town. "I think I see Jomsom."

K.J. sidestepped another rock. "This place brings back memories. Will we be able to get a room?"

"I think so," Emil said. "There's not much traffic here. Besides, who wants to stay in Jomsom?"

Jeff smiled. As they approached the deserted town, the airstrip reminded everyone of the wild helicopter ride.

"I can't wait to get to a room," Mindy said. "I'm afraid to look at my feet."

Emil led them inside the trekking lodge. After checking with the clerk, he announced, "I don't have very good news."

K.J. looked worried. "Uh-oh. Don't tell me the lodge is full."

"No, but the clerk refused to give the uncles and kids a room," Emil explained.

"Why?" Jeff asked.

"They're from a lower caste. But I warned him that if he didn't provide rooms for everybody, we would go somewhere else."

"How do they know who is who?" Mindy asked.

"Just by looking."

K.J. looked puzzled. "If we don't stay here, where would we go?"

Emil laughed. "I don't know. I just told him that we wouldn't stay here!"

"So what are we going to do?" Mindy pressed.

"Well, thankfully, as I thought, he wasn't willing to lose our business. He refused to rent directly to the uncles, but he agreed to give me two rooms and supply us with extra bed frames and mats."

After everyone got settled in the two rooms, Jeff went with Mindy to help her get her boots off.

Mindy lay on the bed. Jeff gently pulled at a boot. "I hope this doesn't hurt," he said, pulling a little harder.

The boot slowly came off. Jeff couldn't believe what he saw: the blisters completely covered the sole of her foot.

Chapter 10

Giant Blisters

Not wanting to alarm his sister, Jeff tried to hide his concern. But Nima's eyes grew big.

Mindy looked nervous. "What's wrong? Is it that bad?"

Jeff didn't want to scare her. "You'll be fine."

"What is it, Nima?" Mindy asked, turning towards her.

Nima shook her head, looking at Jeff.

Mindy twisted one of her feet and caught a glimpse of her raw, red skin. "Oh my goodness. What am I going to do?"

"Did you forget to put the sock liners in?" Jeff asked.

"I haven't worn sock liners yet."

"The liners keep your foot from sliding around in your boot," Jeff said. "No wonder you have so many blisters."

"Am I going to have to fly to Pokhara, too?"

"I don't know. We'll need to spend some time fixing your feet up every day. That's why we have the moleskin."

"How does it look?" Warren asked, limping into the room.

"Not very good," Mindy said. "I forgot to put my sock liners in." She burst into tears. "I've had so many struggles on this trip. But I'm not giving up."

Jeff took his sister's hand.

"Why can't something happen to K.J. and Jeff for once?" Mindy sniffled. "It's not fair."

For the next few minutes, everyone comforted and prayed for Mindy as tears continued to roll down her face. Soon she wiped her eyes and smiled. "Is dinner ready?" she asked, breaking the silence.

Everyone chuckled. Hearing Mindy laugh, Jeff knew she was feeling better.

Warren took a closer look at her foot. "Jeff will have to doctor your feet every night. It will hurt a lot, but you should make it."

"I will make it. I'll make it for the kids."

Jeff lifted one of Mindy's feet and carefully examined it. The blisters started at the edge of her heel and covered the entire sole of her foot. Though many of the blisters were still puffy, a number of them had broken, especially those between her toes.

"Why don't you eat dinner," Jeff said. "Then we'll work on the blisters afterward. It's going to take some time."

Jeff and K.J. carried Mindy to the main dining room and set her down just as the food arrived. Jeff was surprised to see chicken mixed with the curried lentils.

"I've made my decision," Warren announced as they ate. "I'm flying to Pokhara tomorrow morning. I can't be a burden anymore. You guys are in good hands with Emil."

Jeff frowned. "Where will we meet you?"

"If I get treatment for my ankle, I can meet you somewhere along the trail."

"How will you find us?"

Warren laughed. "You guys stick out like a sore thumb. It won't be that hard. Believe me."

"I'll take good care of them," Emil said. "I'm sorry about your ankle."

"God must have a purpose," Warren said. "I thought I would heal. I'll get a hotel room in Pokhara and see what happens." He looked at the team. "Emil will take my place. Watch out for one another."

"We will," Jeff said, feeling a little insecure.

"First, let's take care of Mindy's feet," Warren said. "There won't be any time in the morning."

Jeff and K.J. carried Mindy back to the room and set her down on her sleeping bag. She was in incredible pain.

"I don't think I can take much more," Mindy cried.

Jeff dreaded having to break open every blister.

Warren took Mindy's hand. "They have to be broken open to heal. Otherwise you won't be able to hike tomorrow."

Mindy bit her lip. "Okay."

Jeff worked slowly, first breaking the full blisters

around her toes. Then he wrapped each toe carefully with moleskin.

"Does that stuff really help?" Mindy asked.

Warren nodded. "It creates new skin. It has fuzzy padding on one side and adhesive on the other. The only problem is that when Jeff takes it off, it will hurt."

"Owww," Mindy moaned. "I don't think I want to trek ever again. I thought my feet were in good shape."

"It was the steep downhill with no liners," Warren said gently.

"I'll never forget to use those again."

Jeff covered up his shivering-cold sister with his sleeping bag until only her feet hung out. "I'll be done soon," he told her. "I must do this right."

Tears welled up in Mindy's eyes with each touch. Two hours went by, and everyone else had gone to bed. When Jeff was done, he and Mindy went to sleep exhausted, but confident that Mindy would hike again.

Chapter 11

Hiding in Marpha

Jeff shivered as he peered out the window at the light blanket of fog. He was up early on Friday morning to prepare for the busy day. Warren had to catch the airplane, and the team would begin the trek to Marpha.

Jeff's first priority was to check on Mindy. Nima sat with her, but Mindy didn't have her boots on yet.

"Come on, sis," Jeff urged. "You've got to give it a try."

"I don't know," Mindy said softly. "Maybe I should go with Warren."

Jeff shook his head in disagreement. "Knowing you, I think you'd regret that later."

Mindy nodded, biting her lip. "You're right. I have to try."

Slowly, Jeff helped his sister push her left foot past the opening of the boot. Then the right foot.

Once she had the boots on, Mindy moved her toes. "It still hurts, but the moleskin helps." She stretched her feet out and then stood up.

After praying with her, Jeff headed for breakfast. Nima helped Mindy hobble in.

"Do you think you can make it all day?" Emil asked.

"I think so," Mindy said. "Thanks to Dr. Jeff."

Mindy struggled down the narrow trail. Tears of frustration and pain flowed from her eyes as she muttered scripture verses to herself. Jeff wanted to help her, but knowing how determined she was, he wasn't surprised that she refused help with her backpack. He felt somewhat alone now that Warren had left on the plane.

"I can't believe anybody would sell those kids," Mindy said, amazing Jeff that she could think of anything but her feet. "Goray must be a selfish man."

Emil turned around. "Passang told me he drinks a lot and thinks only of himself."

"It's the story of humanity," Jeff said. "Selfishness."

He felt the wind pick up as they hurried along. Ang Fu and Passang led the way with Chandra and Tenzing on their backs. Jeff knew they could not slow down, since Goray might show up any minute.

"At least it's only six more miles to Marpha," K.J. said.

"I still feel the pain, but I'm learning to block it out," Mindy said, gritting her teeth. "My feet are getting numb."

"You're doing great," Nima encouraged her.

Two hours later, K.J. pointed downward. "I think I spotted Marpha."

Everyone looked down the trail. Sure enough, they could see what appeared to be a town. Walking faster, Jeff noticed that the trail was becoming much narrower, and he realized that Warren wouldn't have made it. Marpha grew larger as the team moved closer.

"I'm excited about seeing the Thakalis people," Jeff said. "Most of them have never heard the name of Jesus. I'm glad we have literature in Nepali."

K.J. looked around in awe. "I wish we could stay awhile. I'd love to get some footage of this place. The mountains look incredible from here."

Jeff hurried to catch up with his best friend. "It's awesome that God can use the footage we get to inspire other Christians to come here. There are so many people groups in the Himalayas who haven't heard about Jesus."

"We won't be able to stay long," Emil said. "Remember, the kids have got to be our priority."

K.J. nodded. "Let's pray for God to open a quick door in Marpha."

Large, recently harvested fields came into view.

"You should see this town right before harvest time," Emil said. "Cabbage, cauliflower, beans, beets, fruits, and grapes—everything flourishes here."

Emil walked a little faster. "The Thakalis are known for their great organization, discipline, cleanliness, and far-sighted vision. With that kind of diligence, they could accomplish great things for God's glory."

Everything they saw was beautiful. Attractive rock walls protected the fields from the deadly wind. Jeff noticed that the village was wedged between steep sandstone cliffs on one side and a small ledge of cultivated fields overlooking the Kali Gandaki on the other. Cobbled alleyways and white-washed mud houses with flat roofs surrounded a number of the courtyards in which livestock were fed. Some of the houses were made of layered white-washed rock with colored shutters on the windows. A stream ran down the middle of the street.

"This is amazing," Mindy said.

Emil pointed to the stream. "That stream is used for everything from drinking water to washing dishes, hair, and feet. It's a wading stream, playpond, watering trough, social center, and town drain."

Donkeys and yaks carried supplies up and down Marpha's main street, while women walked by with baskets of grain strapped to their heads. Small girls carried little kids on their hips. Jeff figured the population here was larger than that of most of the towns they had seen.

"Our church should adopt a people group from Marpha," Mindy said. "We could pray for them daily."

Emil stopped and pointed up a hill. "At the top is the monastery. It's very old and rich."

"Can we take a look?" K.J. asked.

Emil looked at his watch. "If we're careful. We dare not make anyone mad now."

Many people, including Buddhist monks, greeted the team as they headed up the hill. Jeff was surprised by how much stuff was inside the temple: drums, books, masks, prayer wheels, and statues of Buddha.

"I'm getting tired of looking at this stuff," Mindy said. "It represents darkness. This town needs the Light."

That gave Jeff an idea. "Let's see if we can meet a family to tell about Jesus. We need to stay out of sight anyway."

Emil nodded. "Good idea. The kids need a rest. But we must leave Marpha for Larjung by noon."

Jeff looked at his watch. It was about 10:15. With little time to lose, the team hurried back toward town.

"See if anything unusual gets our attention," Jeff suggested.

At the moment Jeff finished speaking, an attractive Nepalese woman walked by selling scarves. She caught everybody's attention, especially Mindy's. She was a young woman, clothed in a bright dress and wrap. Her hair was tied back in a ponytail, and her eyes radiated her natural beauty.

"Emil," Mindy said, "why don't you ask her if we can visit her home. Maybe we can buy some scarves from her."

Emil approached the woman and explained Mindy's request. The woman unfurled a big smile. The team followed her down a cobblestone alley and past two-story houses to a single-story, white-washed house with a flat roof.

The woman stopped and talked to Emil, who translated for the team. "Her name is Kunda. She's inviting us into her home."

Inside, Jeff surveyed the living room. Beautiful paintings depicting the Nepalese lifestyle hung perfectly on different walls. Everything was neat and clean. Jeff saw a statue of Buddha and noticed the tiny dot of red paste on Kunda's forehead.

They sat down on the rattan couches that were covered with cozy, colored pillows. Ang Fu and Passang held on to Chandra and Tenzing as the shy children hid their faces. It wasn't long until Kunda came carrying a tray filled with sodas and another tray piled with fruit and small meat sandwiches.

Everyone was grateful for the short rest. Nima leaned against Mindy. Through Emil's translation, Kunda graciously invited everyone to eat. Emil and the uncles told her about the kids. Jeff could tell by the way she reacted that she was a compassionate woman.

"I've explained to her about your club," Emil said. "I told her you are Christians."

Mindy lit up. "Would you ask her if she is interested in hearing about Jesus?"

Everyone waited for Emil to translate her long answer. Nima, Ang Fu, and Passang listened to every word.

After a few minutes, Emil told the team what Kunda had said. "She says she recently had a vision that confused her."

Everyone leaned forward with interest. Jeff put down his soda.

Kunda used her hands to describe the vision, and Emil translated what she said: "I saw lots of

Hindu gods, Buddha, and even animals being worshiped by our people. After that, I saw a man come up to me with bright and radiant eyes. He told me He was the only path to God. He also said He would send a messenger to help explain the vision."

Jeff felt chills.

Emil went on. "She is wondering if we are the messenger."

The team sat in amazement. Jeff was still trying to process what he had just heard. Out of all the people in Marpha, he still couldn't believe how they had met this woman.

"I believe we are the messenger," Jeff said. "God is so amazing."

"He is," Emil said. "He wants us to share with her."

Mindy and K.J. prayed as Jeff turned to Kunda. He began to share through Emil's translation. "One of our main purposes in coming to Nepal is to share about the only pathway to God. The person in your vision is named Jesus. He is God's only Son, and He came to earth two thousand years ago to bring hope and life to everyone."

The uncles leaned forward.

Jeff felt the presence of God as he continued. "Jesus came to show us the way. That way can't be found in lifeless idols or false gods. Jesus is the living God."

Kunda's eyes moistened with tears. Jeff saw light filling her eyes. He continued sharing for the next thirty minutes, explaining the gospel story from creation to the coming of Christ. Kunda hung on every word and couldn't wait for the translation. Passang and Ang Fu hardly blinked.

Later, Jeff asked Mindy to share. Wiping her eyes, Mindy opened her heart and shared of God's amazing love, and how Jesus died once to allow humankind to live forever.

"All you have to do is ask Him into your heart." Emil translated. "He will come in and live forever."

Jeff was impressed with Mindy's ability to bring closure to the message. Mindy led Kunda in prayer. Kunda's face shone as she lifted her head. At that very moment, Jeff remembered his deep desire to see God's glory come to Nepal, and he knew his prayer was being answered.

Kunda shared for the next few minutes. "This message is the true message," Emil translated. "It must be given to the Thakalis. Please stay for a few days so you can share this story with everyone."

"Tell her we must leave because of the kids, but we'll send a team back to visit her," Mindy responded.

"Yes!" K.J. said. "This is why we make the videos." He reached for his camera. In his excitement, he turned to speak to Kunda directly. "Kunda, will you share a little bit about your people and your story on video so that believers in our country can pray for the Thakalis?"

Emil explained to Kunda what Mindy and K.J. had said, and Kunda agreed happily.

When she had finished, Jeff reached into his backpack and pulled out a Nepali Bible. "Please take this," he told Kunda as he handed it to her. "The words will change your life."

Tears welled up in Kunda's eyes as she took the Bible and hugged it.

Jeff felt overwhelmed. "We'll never forget you."

"Please pray for my people," Kunda pleaded.

"We will," K.J. promised. "And so will a lot of other people when they hear what you've shared today."

"Tell her we still want to buy some scarves," Mindy said.

"The scarves are gifts from me," Kunda protested when Emil had translated Mindy's request. "You have given me the greatest gift I could ever have. Thank you for what you have done." Kunda smiled as she passed out scarves to everyone.

Emil looked at his watch. It was just before noon. Emil promised Kunda that he would come back to visit, and after exchanging addresses, everyone gave her a hug, even Ang Fu and Passang, who were wiping tears from their eyes.

Walking down an alleyway with Kunda, the team headed to the main trail, with Tenzing and Chandra on their uncles' backs. Before they could go far, Ang Fu stopped and spoke to Emil in a frantic manner.

Emil's jaw dropped as he stared down the road. "Goray is right in front of us," he warned.

Chapter 12

Trekking on Slippery Ground

Look!" K.J. cried in astonishment. "He's talking with those New Jersey guys."

"Shawn and Jay said they knew him," Jeff said. "Maybe they decided to travel down with him."

"All I know is that we need to leave now," Emil said.

Emil quickly explained the situation to Kunda. Nima translated for the team as Emil and Kunda hurriedly made plans. "She knows a way out where we won't be seen. She has some friends who can divert them for a while."

As the team hid behind a wall, Kunda left to contact her friends. When she came back, her eyes still beamed with new life. She said something in Nepali, and Jeff felt frustrated not understanding. No one had time to explain.

Leading the team through a dry field, Kunda zigzagged her way to the main trail.

Jeff looked back and saw a policeman in a green uniform talking to Goray, Shawn, and Jay. "What is she saying?" he asked Nima.

"She promised that the men will be detained for a little while," Nima translated.

Jeff recognized Emil and Kunda thanking each other in Nepali. Both had reason to be grateful. Then, with smiles and waves to their new friend, Emil led the team down the trail, away from Kunda and the Thakalis. But Jeff knew that their hearts and prayers were still in Marpha even as their feet carried them toward Larjung.

The team hiked as fast as they could. The lower they trekked, the greener the trail became. Every few minutes, Jeff turned and looked back.

"Goray will catch us, won't he?" Jeff asked.

Emil raised his chin a bit. "Probably. But the farther we get from his home, the more likely he might be to give up. He knows he can't carry those kids alone."

K.J. shuddered. "Unless he hires two friendly helpers."

For a moment, everyone pondered that thought, then pushed it to the back of their minds, hoping it wasn't true.

"The trails get narrow through here," Emil said. "Let's take the lower trail near the river as long as we can. If that doesn't work, we'll have to hike the higher one."

The team was in too much of a hurry to notice the incredible beauty, although K.J. continued to look at their surroundings through his photographer's eye. Finally, they sat down near the river for a rest.

"This river is beautiful," Jeff said, watching the rushing water. "No wonder things are so green."

"The snowpack creates lots of spring water," Emil explained.

"I wish I could drink some of it," K.J. said. "I'm tired of iodine tablets in my water. I can't wait to get back to the good ol' U.S.A."

Everyone laughed. Jeff and Mindy knew what it was like to miss home, but they also knew that none of them—least of all K.J.—would trade their adventures for convenience.

Mindy turned to Jeff as if a light had switched on in her head. "No wonder we've had such a battle. Enduring blisters doesn't seem like such a big deal after seeing Kunda come to Jesus."

Jeff pushed a branch out of their way. "That meeting with Kunda was so incredible. Her vision totally blew my mind."

"It was very humbling to be her messenger," Mindy said. "God sent us to her."

Nima turned to Mindy. "I don't think God sent you just to her. As I listened to you share, a lot of stuff became clear to me."

Jeff slowed the pace a bit. He knew it was a very special moment. Emil's eyes filled with tears.

Nima looked right at Mindy, her eyes misty. "Since I was abandoned by both of my parents when I was a baby, I always thought I had done something evil in a previous life." Nima wiped her eyes and went on. "I hated all those girls' homes I had to live in. I felt like a piece of trash."

They all stopped.

Nima looked at Emil. "That's why I didn't want you to adopt Tenzing and Chandra. I wanted to be the only one in the house. I was tired of being just a number."

Nima fell to her knees, no longer able to control her tears. Mindy wrapped her arms around her as Emil, Jeff, and K.J. knelt beside them. Ang Fu and Passang didn't know what to do. Several trekkers stopped, wondering what was going on. Emil assured them that everything was okay.

Nima looked up. "I want God to be my Father. I want Jesus to live in my heart."

During the next few minutes, Mindy led Nima in a prayer as Emil quietly wept.

After Mindy finished, Nima looked up through her tears. "I know that God loves me and that I am special, no matter what the caste system says. He even has a purpose for my life. I have such a new joy in my heart for those kids. I want them to be rescued by love, just as I was. They're going to be my brother and sister."

The group rejoiced together. Jeff's heart was so full that he wouldn't trade what he felt at that moment for all the money in the world.

After a pause, the team trekked down. Nima had Chandra on her back while Mindy carried Tenzing and the uncles carried the backpacks. They hiked down rugged terrain along trails so narrow they had to wait for others to pass. Rocks were slippery with green moss. The trees became larger and greener.

Mindy looked at Emil. "I think I need a little rest. Maybe we should let the uncles carry the kids again."

Nima nodded in agreement, and the group sat down for a rest.

"I wonder what those police did to delay Goray," K.J. said.

Emil shook his head in amazement. "I don't know, but Kunda had to be an angel from heaven."

After a few moments, everyone got up and followed Emil down. They needed to be in Larjung before dark.

Straight ahead was a large suspension bridge over the rushing river.

"That's cool," K.J. said. "But it's a long way down."

Mindy was the first to make note of the narrow walkway. "This bridge isn't very wide."

"I don't like this thing," Jeff admitted as he stepped onto the moving bridge. "It's awfully shaky."

Mindy began to panic when she saw a man about halfway across leading some yaks toward them. "There's not enough room. I'm going back," she cried. "Those yaks will knock us into the river."

Jeff looked ahead. "We can make it. Just stay out of their way."

Slowly, the team approached the yaks. Emil went first, followed by the uncles and then Nima. Mindy was terrified. She trembled with every step. The yak owner yelled at her in Nepali as she slipped by. As Jeff and K.J. tried to pass, the owner's grip on the reins loosened. A large yak started to charge after them.

"Run back, K.J.!" Jeff cried. Just then, the angry yak smashed into Jeff's side. With nowhere else to move, he was pushed up against the rope railing.

K.J. ran back to the side they had started from, clutching his camera bag in terror.

"Help!" Jeff screamed.

The yak threw its head back and forth. Jeff knew he had no other choice. He quickly climbed over the rope siding, hanging on for dear life. This was safer than being crushed or thrown off the bridge.

Emil was yelling at the owner. Mindy prayed aloud for safety.

"Hold on tight! Don't fall!" Nima cried.

Everyone was praying now. Jeff tried to balance his feet on the tiny ledge of wood. The yak was getting angrier, and it crashed into the ropes again. Jeff lost his footing. Falling toward the river, he held on to the rope siding and dangled there. Suspended in midair, he felt his hand slowly slipping. He swung back and forth as the bridge was jostled.

At last Emil got the yak owner to move the animals away. "Hold on, Jeff," he called. "I'll pull you up by your belt."

Ang Fu and Passang helped Emil while Mindy and Nima clutched the crying children. Emil leaned over the rope siding. Raging white water splashed against the sharp rocks. Jeff was panicking, but he knew not to look down. Emil had one chance to get Jeff. Reaching down, he grabbed Jeff's belt and gripped it tightly. Jeff still dangled as Emil slowly pulled him up.

Seconds later, Jeff was back on the edge. He put his feet down and quickly climbed over the rope siding. Collapsing onto the suspension bridge, Jeff gasped for air.

"Let's get off this thing," Emil said as the team headed for solid ground.

❖❖❖❖❖❖❖

As the group approached Larjung, the river got wider and shallower. Jeff noticed the gravel bars interlacing the divided streams. A few pine, fir, and sweet-smelling cedar trees appeared, thickening as the landscape became greener. Moss grew on the granite. It was as if they were entering a different world.

"It's pretty in here," Mindy said. "This is my kind of hiking."

"And it's getting warmer," Nima added.

"Just keep me away from any yaks!" Mindy exclaimed.

"Me, too," Jeff cried.

The team arrived in Larjung at seven p.m. A monastery appeared, a handful of flags flying from the roof. It was perched on a low hill between the town and the river. Jeff admired the beauty of the elegantly carved wooden beams typical of Tibetan houses and courtyard stables.

Mindy shivered. "I thought we were moving into warmer air."

"Not when the wind swirls," Emil said.

"What exactly are those prayer flags at the top of the temple?" Jeff asked. "I've seen them almost everywhere."

"I read about them while researching Buddhism," Mindy explained. "People believe that these multicolored flags send prayers to the gods. They write Buddhist scriptures or prayers on them and then fly them from high places. Sometimes they even just throw them into the wind."

The frayed prayer flags snapped on tall poles. After countless prayers had been wind-whipped to Buddha, Jeff could understand why they had turned to rags. The writing was hardly readable.

"Larjung is eighty-four hundred feet high," Emil said, seeing Mindy still shivering. "That can keep things a bit cold."

"Not as cold as Muktinath," Mindy reminded them. "That was beyond cold."

Ang Fu and Passang laughed after Emil translated. Muktinath, after all, was home.

Soon Emil spotted a trekking lodge. After a nice meal and some needed warmth around the table, an exhausted Jeff was grateful for Nima's support as he tended Mindy's blisters. Mindy became almost sick with pain as Jeff pulled off the moleskin, especially when skin came off with it. For his sister's sake, Jeff remained calm, even though the job wasn't pleasant. Tomorrow he and Mindy would each need to be ready for another day's hike. Tonight Jeff was just glad to be alive.

❖❖❖❖❖❖❖

The alarm sounded at five a.m. The team ate a quick breakfast and planned their trek to Ghasa. Around 5:30, they headed for the trail. Though it was still dark, it wouldn't be long until the sun's early rays would overtake the night.

"This should be a shorter hike today," Emil said.

"My feet would like to thank you," Mindy smiled. "I don't know if I can handle another moleskin change."

Nima hugged Mindy as they walked on. The trail got incredibly steep and difficult to negotiate.

Emil looked below and noticed that some of the trail was missing. Quickly, he stopped everyone. "It could be really dangerous down there. A part of the trail has been wiped out. Hold on to a branch to keep your balance."

The whole hillside was a moving mass of mud, water, and moss. Jeff slowly put his foot forward, only to discover that he was ankle deep in mud. He took a second step. He sunk in knee-deep. "This is unbelievable."

"I'm not going in that," K.J. cried. "That's gross."

"We have to," Emil said. "We can't turn around."

Slogging one foot ahead of the other, everyone was quickly covered with thick muck.

"We're almost through," Jeff said. "Just keep going."

As Jeff spoke, a branch that K.J. was holding broke. He lost his balance and went sprawling over the muddy mountainside, screaming. Jeff carefully hurried to the edge to look and saw K.J. hanging from a large branch above the river. Terror filled his best friend's eyes.

Chapter 13

Trouble Brewing at the Hot Springs

Keep a good grip, K.J.," Jeff cried. "We'll get you."

"You'll have to give me your hand," Emil said.

"I'm not letting go," K.J. protested. "I'll fall and drown."

"This is where trust comes in," Jeff said. "I'm your best friend, and I won't let you drown. Come on."

Jeff gripped Emil's waist so that the experienced guide could reach down farther. Slowly, Emil tugged on K.J. until finally he crawled over the edge.

K.J. stomped mud and water out of his boots. "It'll be a miracle if we get home," K.J. said. "This is

Mindy's fault. She wished all that suffering stuff on both of us."

Mindy snapped. "It's not my fault you can't watch where you're going. And besides, why should I be the one to fight all the battles?"

"Hey, you guys," Jeff jumped in before K.J. could respond. "The enemy knows that the best way to prevent us from sharing the gospel is to destroy our unity. The best way to fight back is to forgive one another and work as a team. I know you guys can do it; you've done it before!"

Now was not the time for the team to fall apart.

❖❖❖❖❖❖❖

Hours later, they were cautiously balanced on a cliff path fifteen hundred feet above the water. Emil had decided to move the team to the higher, dryer trail. At one point, this trail narrowed to three feet wide—so narrow that they could barely get their backpacks through the brush.

"How do these yaks and donkey trains get by here?" Jeff asked.

"I don't know," Mindy said. "But I wish we were back in that riverbed near Jomsom. At least there the trail was fairly straight."

Emil pulled Nima through a narrow spot. "The hardest thing to decide is which side of the river to hike on."

"We seem to always be on the wrong side," K.J. said.

"Would you like my job?" Emil asked with a grin.

"No, sir. I'm with you all the way."

Jeff looked at his watch as they paused to rest. He was glad it was almost five. He didn't feel very well. As they approached Ghasa, Jeff felt a sharp pain in his stomach. By the time they arrived at the trekking lodge, Jeff could barely walk. Pain raced up and down his stomach.

"Something has hit me like a bomb," Jeff said to Mindy. "I'm going to bed. Emil and Nima will have to fix your feet."

Jeff couldn't wait for Emil to check them in. He got out his sleeping bag. The smell of the food sitting on the table made him feel like throwing up. He tossed his sleeping bag on the floor, kicked it open, and crawled in. The cramps became worse, and he doubled over in pain.

The team gathered around him and prayed. Jeff was exhausted, but he couldn't go to sleep, so he headed for the bathroom. He felt like he was going to be really sick.

Eventually, Jeff drifted into a restless sleep, and as the Sunday morning rays warmed him, he felt for his stomach. Every bit of pain was gone. Smiling, he looked around for someone he could tell about his restored health.

"Anybody out there?" Jeff asked. "Hello?"

"It's good to hear your voice," Emil said. "We didn't know if you would make it. I almost called a doctor."

"In order for me to be as hungry as I am now, God must have healed me. How was the food last night?"

K.J. rolled over. "It gets better as we go. You can even order stuff on the menu and actually get it."

Jeff put on his hiking boots and headed for breakfast. Everybody soon joined him, including the uncles and kids.

Jeff examined the menu. "I thought you said there were more choices."

"I meant for dinner," K.J. laughed.

Nima picked up Tenzing and set him on her lap. Chandra was still a little shy as Mindy tried to play with her.

"I wonder if Goray gave up," Jeff said. It's strange we haven't run into him."

Emil nodded. "Tonight we'll be in Tatopani."

Mindy smiled. "I can't believe it. I've been looking forward to the day when I can finally get a bath."

"I've been looking forward to it, too," K.J. teased.

"Watch it," Mindy said. "You're the one that's going to turn the water brown."

❖❖❖❖❖❖❖

The team left the subalpine zone and entered the subtropics as they headed toward Tatopani. Lizards skittered around in the dust. Jeff marveled at the different kind of beauty he saw, like the orange trees that began to appear.

K.J. looked ahead. "It's a checkpoint," he said with worry.

"That's not just a checkpoint," Emil said, hurrying the pace. "It's also a village. This is a large and long town called Dana. We'll get something to drink here."

Everybody cheered for the chance to rest.

As usual, the agents examined the trekking permits before signing each of them. One of the agents spoke to Emil and the uncles. It sounded to Jeff as if something was wrong. He was anxious to hear Emil's explanation.

After a little while, Emil and the uncles joined the team.

"What's wrong?" Mindy asked.

"The agent told us that three men were here yesterday. He said they were asking questions about us. Two of them were Americans."

"When did they come through?"

"Yesterday evening."

"Looks like we're following them," Mindy said.

"That's okay," K.J. assured them. "We'll keep an eye on those guys."

"I wish it was that easy," Emil said, looking nervous. "No telling where they'll show up. Goray will make a move for the kids sometime."

After a cool drink, the team headed down the trail. Jeff trusted God, but he could feel the tension building.

After several hours, Jeff figured they must be getting close to Tatopani. The trail opened up, and wild marigolds appeared everywhere. Pears and potatoes grew nearby. As they passed a small poinsettia farm, he remembered that Christmas was just five days away. Chickens mingled in the streets with cats and dogs, and a donkey caravan passed.

K.J. walked in step with Emil as they carefully crossed a bridge. "Tell me about Tatopani."

"Tatopani means 'hot springs,'" Emil began. "The altitude is only four thousand feet and very pleasant. Everybody loves to stop here."

"How big are the hot springs?"

"About the size of a swimming pool. Not an Olympic size pool, but big."

"How is the water?"

Emil grinned. "It's just what your body needs after a hike like this!"

Jeff couldn't wait.

Soon they were headed for the trekking lodge. The streets of Tatopani were paved with large flagstones. Everything looked clean and modern.

At first the clerk at the lodge refused to check them in. Jeff wondered if the disagreement had to do with the uncles' caste. He couldn't understand Nepali, but he could tell that Emil was speaking strongly to the clerk, and finally the two shook hands.

Making their way to their rooms, the tired and dirty team had one thing in mind: bathing in the hot springs. Jeff remembered, however, that he needed to check Mindy's feet before she could go in. He pulled her boot off.

"Take it easy, Jeff," Mindy said, wincing a little. "We covered a lot of trail today."

First the boots came off, then the socks.

"It's looking better," Jeff encouraged her. "Let's wrap a couple toes and your heel. It'll be well soon."

"Will I be able to go in the hot springs?"

"Who can keep you out? But wear your sandals."

"Then let's go!" Mindy jumped up.

Just minutes after getting into the hot springs, every muscle in Jeff's body was already grateful for the natural hot water. The springs were even better than Emil had described. The natural pool was waist deep and surrounded by rocks of every size and shape. The backdrop was a blend of beautiful green trees and high rocky mountains against an absolutely clear sky. Except for a few soap containers and pieces of trash strewn along the shore, it was a perfect place.

"This is like bath water," Mindy said. "I've waited a long time for this moment."

"God is good," Jeff smiled. "We've come a long way."

K.J. finally stopped filming and slipped into the pool.

Jeff stretched. "I wish Warren could be here. It's not the same without him."

Mindy splashed some water at her brother. "I know. He would have really enjoyed meeting Kunda and relaxing in these hot springs."

Jeff watched the other trekkers sitting around the springs. They were from all over the world. Then, looking toward the trekking lodge, Jeff's heartbeat quickened. Coming toward them down the pathway were Shawn and Jay.

Jeff had a sinking feeling that Goray wouldn't be far behind.

Chapter 14

Warning

Jeff looked for Goray but couldn't see him. Taking a deep breath, he prepared for a possible confrontation with the brothers.

Shawn came into the water and startled K.J. with a splash. "How's it going?"

K.J. backed up, surprised. He stared at Shawn. "Great," he said warily.

Mindy moved close to Jeff and whispered, "Where are Chandra and Tenzing?"

"The uncles are with them. They're taking a nap. Emil and Nima are back at the lodge, too."

"I hope the kids are okay," Mindy said. "Let's see what these guys want."

Jay pulled off his T-shirt. After wading into the water, he headed toward Jeff. "We would like to talk to you about something."

"Sure," Jeff agreed.

Mindy and K.J. listened closely.

"What do you really know about Emil?" Jay asked.

"He came highly recommended as a guide."

"What about this adoption thing?" Shawn asked.

"He has legal adoption papers."

"We know Goray pretty well," Shawn said, "and he has accused Emil of kidnapping the kids. He thinks Emil manipulated the whole thing. He believes the papers aren't legal. He's pretty upset. He'll probably take Emil to court."

Mindy didn't like what she was hearing. She came to Emil's defense. "Emil is an honest man. His family will make a wonderful home for Tenzing and Chandra."

"You guys seem pretty determined to help those kids, so we hope you're doing the right thing by helping Emil." Jay sounded doubtful.

Jeff's heart was pounding. "We think we are."

"We heard you guys stopped in Marpha," Shawn pried.

"We visited a woman there," K.J. volunteered.

"She has some police friends, doesn't she?"

"We only met her for the first time," Jeff said.

Shawn lay back in the water. "Oh."

Jeff didn't want to beat around the bush anymore. "Look. We know these kids' lives are at stake. Do you know where Goray is?"

Shawn looked over at Jay. "We think he's headed to Kathmandu."

"We thought you guys were staying in Muktinath for a few days."

"We were going to, but some of our money got stolen. We had to head down the mountain."

"I'm sorry that happened."

"We are, too," Jay said.

Jeff looked over at Mindy and K.J. "We should be going now. We'll see you guys," he said as the three got out of the water.

Jay followed them to the edge of the pool. "Don't get too involved in this mess. The police might end up arresting you if you're wrong about Emil. Kidnapping is a serious charge."

As the team headed along the path to the lodge, the conversation with Shawn and Jay rang in Jeff's ears. He felt confused, but he knew Emil was a good man.

"We didn't kidnap anybody," Mindy said as they walked along the flagstone pathway. "Those kids legally belong to Emil and Mary Anne."

"We know that," Jeff said, "but Goray must have told them a convincing story."

"Yeah," K.J. snorted. "I wonder if he stole their money, too!"

At the lodge, the team explained to Emil everything Shawn and Jay had said.

Emil looked worried. "Goray is a good storyteller."

"Do you think those guys really believe we kidnapped the kids?" Jeff asked.

"They've got the story all messed up," K.J. said.

"They do," Emil confirmed. "But I'm not concerned with what Shawn and Jay think, just with where Goray is. I'll inform Ang Fu and Passang. The rest of you—don't let this interfere with your relaxing time. Tomorrow will be the hardest hike we have had. The trip to Ghoripani Pass is a vertical mile uphill, spread over six miles."

Mindy didn't want to hear that. "You mean we have to go up again?"

"That's right," Emil said. "That's why I planned this rest time. We all have to be strong to get these kids off the mountain and home to Mary Anne."

Jeff and K.J. nodded in agreement.

Mindy changed the subject. "I just want a real bath. Now."

"There's hot water here at the lodge," Emil reminded her. "You can bathe for as long as you want."

"Are the kids still sleeping?" Jeff asked.

"Yes. So are the uncles. They're exhausted."

"Don't you think they'll want to go in the hot springs with the kids?" Mindy asked.

"I don't think it's a good idea now," Emil said. "They feel embarrassed to go in because of..." he hesitated.

"Because of the caste system," Mindy interjected. "I think it stinks."

"They plan on going tomorrow morning at daybreak, right before we leave."

"Good," Mindy said. "It'll be good for them."

"We need to be alert," Emil said.

"We will," Jeff promised. "I just wonder where Goray is. Why hasn't he shown up?"

Emil shrugged. "Maybe he still will. Or maybe he went on down the mountain. He might try to take it to court. I'll have to face that then."

❖❖❖❖❖❖❖

Jeff had never been so excited to do laundry.

"I can't believe I've worn these clothes for this long," Jeff said, wrinkling his nose. "The water is filthy."

K.J. laughed. "My clothes could stand up by themselves."

Emil overheard them and smiled. "You'll never again take for granted the great conveniences you have in America, will you?"

"That's for sure," Jeff said. "I'll always be grateful for running water."

Just then, they heard a knock. Emil went to get it. Jeff felt a little jumpy, anxious that Shawn and Jay may have told Goray where to find them. He waited and listened. Relieved, he heard Mindy's voice from the other room.

"Are you guys dressed?" Mindy called.

"Yes," Jeff called back. "Come in."

"I wasn't sure if you guys were taking a bath."

"We're washing our clothes," K.J. said, kneeling by the bathtub. "You should see this water."

"No thanks." Mindy made a face. "My bath water was dirty enough. Where are Chandra and Tenzing?"

"In their room," Emil said. "I was able to get them a room with the uncles. But it doesn't have a tub."

Mindy was bewildered. "You mean those kids haven't had a bath?"

"No," Emil said. "They were going to do that in the springs tomorrow morning."

"They should have a real bath," Mindy said. "Do you mind if Nima and I give them one?"

Emil looked up from his washing. "I think that would be wonderful."

A little later, Ang Fu and Passang carried the two dirty kids to Mindy and Nima. Chandra was still fearful, even as Mindy lifted her into her arms. The small girl started to cry.

"It's okay," Mindy cooed. "I'm going to make you feel better."

Jeff stayed in the room as Mindy got the bath water to the perfect temperature.

Nima put the kids into the old-style four-legged tub and started scrubbing. "Here we go." Tenzing smiled and splashed Nima as she bathed him.

After a while, Mindy fought back tears. "These kids have known lots of rejection. It's hard to believe Goray could think of selling them. God's heart must break when He sees children treated like this."

Mindy dried the children off and combed their hair. Jeff felt blessed to see Mindy's love in action and was also touched by how God had brought so much love into Nima's heart. He knew that it was at moments like these that a little bit more of God's light shined in Nepal.

❖❖❖❖❖❖❖

The alarm clock announced the new day at five a.m. It was Monday, December 21. Jeff's aching body affirmed that they had been trekking for six days. Wanting to muster up all the energy he could for the Ghoripani Pass hike, Jeff was hoping for a good breakfast. He met the others at the breakfast table, and they all filled up on rolls and cereal. K.J. kept exclaiming over the choice of food, making everyone laugh.

"I'll bet the uncles are having a good time with the kids at the hot springs," Mindy exclaimed.

"They didn't take them," Emil said. "You did such a good job bathing them. We decided it would be better to let them sleep."

"We should wake them soon," Mindy suggested.

Jeff could see that his sister wanted to be with the kids. He also knew it would be hard for her to leave them in a few days.

Emil thought about what she said. "We'll let them sleep fifteen minutes more. Passang and Ang Fu should be back by then."

Jeff noticed that breakfast was especially nice this morning. Yesterday's bath had lifted everybody's spirits.

After a while, Mindy looked at her watch. "It's been fifteen minutes. I'm going to get those little munchkins." Mindy excused herself and headed down the hall to the kids' room. The rest of the team started discussing the hike.

Suddenly, they were startled by a loud scream. Jeff jumped out of his seat. What had happened to his sister?

Mindy ran back in the room in a panic. "The kids are gone!"

Chapter 15

The Vertical Mile

Jeff didn't believe his ears. His mind raced wildly. "Passang and Ang Fu must have decided to take the kids to the hot springs anyway."

"Let's check," Emil said.

Mindy ran to the door with Nima beside her. Just then, Passang and Ang Fu walked in—without the kids. Emil quickly questioned them, and they ran to where the kids had been sleeping. Moments later, the three rushed out.

Emil looked sick. "They've been taken all right."

"What are we going to do?" Mindy asked. "How could we let this happen?"

"We'll find them," Jeff said. "We shouldn't have stopped here."

Passang and Ang Fu sat down, looking very sad. Ang Fu put his face in his hands.

"Tell them it's not their fault," Jeff said.

"Let's go to the police," K.J. suggested. "They can put the word out up and down the trail."

"We don't know which way they went," Jeff said. "Don't you think Goray would head up the mountain?"

"Not if he was going to make money on them," Emil countered. "He'll take them to Kathmandu."

"Wouldn't they be spotted on the trail?" Jeff asked.

"Not if he hides them. Since they're so little, he can wrap them in a blanket. He could even put them in a basket. All he has to do is give them a sleeping pill."

Mindy's face filled with rage. "I can't handle this talk. Let's do something."

"First," Jeff said, "let's ask God to help us."

They all agreed and bowed their heads. "Lord Jesus," Jeff prayed, "thank You that You sent us to rescue these kids. Someone has taken them. Please help us find them. We need Your wisdom now. Amen."

Everyone stood for a moment in silence.

"Should we go to the police?" Mindy asked.

"It would be good to alert them," Emil agreed. "But I don't know how much they can do."

The team made their way to the station. Emil, Ang Fu, and Passang explained the situation to the police while the others continued to pray.

Emil and the uncles became more and more excited as they spoke to the police.

Emil came over to explain. "God has answered our prayers! The policemen told us that on their patrols they ran into two American hikers who were asking about a man and two kids headed to Kathmandu. I'm sure they meant Goray, and Ang Fu and Passang also think that's where he's headed."

"That's great news!" K.J. beamed.

"At least now we know which way to go," Mindy said.

"I knew we wouldn't lose them," K.J. cheered with his usual confidence.

The team went back to the lodge to discuss what would happen next. It was almost eight a.m.

"I think we need to go to Ghoripani," Emil said. "He has to go through there if he's going to Kathmandu. But he's got a good head start on us."

"Those two American hikers must have been Shawn and Jay, which means they knew he took the kids. I bet they're helping Goray," K.J. said.

Emil shrugged. "It's hard to say. They could be, if they've been deceived by him."

As he spoke, a young Nepalese boy ran into the room. He had a note in his hand that he gave to Emil. After reading it, Emil dropped his shoulders.

"What is it?" Mindy pleaded.

"It's a note from Goray."

"What does it say?" Jeff asked.

Emil held up the note. "Goray says that the kids are his responsibility, since he is one of the closest relatives."

"That's all?" Mindy asked. "Read the rest of it."

"Don't try to find the kids," Emil read. "Your adoption papers won't hold up. I am the only relative who was willing to take them. They will be fine with me. I am sorry for all your trouble, but stay away."

Mindy dropped into a chair. Jeff's mouth was still wide open.

"He can't do that, can he?" K.J. asked.

"We weren't going to adopt them until January 15, when the adoption is final. That's why he wanted to get the kids now."

"Do you think he'll still try to sell them?" Jeff asked.

"The uncles are sure that's what he wants to do."

"Will he still go to Kathmandu?" Mindy asked.

"I'm sure of it."

"And I bet Shawn and Jay are helping him carry the kids," Jeff said.

Everyone nodded in dismay.

"Goray can't make it to Kathmandu by tonight," K.J. said.

"He doesn't have to go all the way," Emil stated. "He has connections in Ghoripani. He'll make a deal and pay somebody else to take them down. Besides, he can move pretty fast if those two brothers are with him."

Emil discussed with Passang and Ang Fu what had just happened. Turning to the rest of the group, he told them, "Goray has made many trips to Kathmandu. Passang said the whole family has suspicions of his dealings there."

"What should we do?" Jeff asked. "We can't let him go through with it."

"If we can catch up with him, we could offer to buy the kids ourselves," Mindy offered. "I've got some money in savings. We could wire it over."

"That's very generous of you, Mindy. My wife would give anything to get those kids. But I hate to give in to his greed."

"It doesn't matter," Mindy countered. "Those kids' lives are worth everything in the world. We can do it. We just have to catch up before he sells them."

Nima hugged Mindy. "Thanks, Mindy."

"Let's catch up with them first," K.J. suggested. "God will show us what to do then. I'm willing to help."

Emil was discouraged. "I don't think we can catch up. The police said they would put the word out. But even if they find him, they can't do anything until the adoption is final."

Jeff sighed. "I'd feel better if Warren were here. He would know what to do."

"I'd feel better, too," Mindy said. "But K.J. is right. God will show us what to do."

"Let's alert the police on the way out about the note," Emil said.

"We'll never see those kids again if we don't hurry," Jeff said.

Mindy shook her head. "Remember, we prayed," she reminded them.

❖❖❖❖❖❖❖

After spending some time at the police station, everyone agreed that they should head to Ghoripani.

Strapping their backpacks on, the discouraged team started out. Passang and Ang Fu decided to trek as far as Ghoripani.

As they climbed higher, the scenery grew more and more spectacular. Thick moss hung off huge trees. Primroses sent their curled, bright shoots up from underfoot. A jasmine-like smell filled the air, and a number of screeching squirrels raised their tails at the trekkers. The colorful Himalayan pied woodpecker hammered away on a nearby tree. Along the trail, people looked healthier and more well-off.

"What time do you think we'll get there?" Jeff asked.

Emil looked at his watch. It was already noon. "Close to nine if we continue at this fast pace."

Mindy trekked on with determination. "I should have stayed with those kids."

"Nobody is to blame," Jeff said. "They were right down the hall."

A few moments later, Emil stopped. "Does anyone need a break?"

Mindy quickly shook her head. "We have one chance to get those kids. Let's keep moving."

"Maybe Goray will be stopped at one of the checkpoints," K.J. hoped.

Emil stared walking again. "I got the impression that the agents aren't going to be too concerned about kids from a lower caste."

"I hate the caste system," Mindy said. "I wish people could see as God sees and understand how valuable each person is."

Emil heartily agreed with her and quickened the pace. Jeff was almost out of breath as he tried to keep up. They were racing against the clock, and they knew the powers of darkness would fight them every step of the way.

"Is this pace okay?" Emil asked.

"I can't keep this up all day," K.J. groaned. "My back is killing me."

"My legs are about to fall off," Mindy said. "But I'm not giving up. I've learned to handle suffering on this trip."

Breathing harder, K.J. gathered determination. Jeff continued to push himself. He knew he couldn't give in to his desire for comfort, either. His mind was flooded with images of Jesus trekking to Calvary.

Jeff turned to Mindy. "I've just been thinking about Jesus. He had to trek up the toughest mountain and carry a cross with Him. He totally denied Himself. He knew what suffering was all about."

"I've been thinking the same thing," Mindy said. "I'm ashamed of my constant desire for comfort and fun. The world will never be won without a struggle." She paused. "I'm not giving in this time."

"I'm proud of you, Mindy."

Mindy smiled with new determination.

After almost ten hours of hiking, the group came to a village. Jeff saw men and women cutting grain. Others were beating millet on large woven mats in walled courtyards. Children swept it into piles. Ragged sheep and goats grazed nearby.

Emil pointed up a long embankment of steps. "Straight ahead is Ghoripani Pass."

Jeff looked and saw a series of worn, rounded steps about four to six feet wide zigzagging up and down the valley floor.

"I don't think I have ever hiked from Tatopani to Ghoripani Pass in such a short time," Emil commented.

"That's because we're focused," Mindy said.

Getting closer, Jeff saw the town. The buildings here looked different to Jeff from those in the other towns. "What's wrong with those buildings?"

Emil laughed. "The construction here is totally different than in Marpha. The buildings are a little crooked."

Jeff shook his head as he scanned the buildings. Nothing looked square. The streets were crowded with horses, mules, yaks, donkey trains, trekkers, and rickshaws fighting for space.

Emil soon found a trekking lodge. "It will be nine o'clock soon. Let's check in."

"I'm hungry," K.J. said. "Let's eat something."

Jeff smiled.

Mindy laughed. "So much for suffering."

K.J. ignored her comment. After checking into the lodge, the team waited in the dining area.

"We should get something to eat," Emil said. "Then we'll try to find Goray."

Mindy was reluctant, but like everyone else she was totally exhausted from the long hike. Thirty minutes went by, and Mindy's frustration grew with each passing second. Everyone was hungry and discouraged. When the food arrived, K.J. devoured the rice and chicken as if he hadn't eaten in days.

After dinner, they asked questions of people around the lodge. No one seemed to know anything. Moving outside, they saw an older gentleman sitting on a bench. After a quick discussion, Emil turned back to the team.

"He saw them come through here earlier. Three adults carrying a couple of kids. He said that two of them were Americans."

"Does he know where they are?"

"He thinks they left already."

Chapter 16

The True Circle of Life

They've got to be in Ghoripani," Mindy cried. "Let's search for them."

"Goray is smarter than that," Emil said. "He's probably camping out somewhere nearby; it's not as cold around here. We'll have to wait until morning."

Everyone agreed and bowed their heads as K.J. prayed. "Lord, we need an answer. Please help us find the kids. Please protect them from being sold."

After the prayer, Jeff looked up and saw the woman who ran the lodge staring at them. Emil noticed it, too, and asked her if anything was wrong Emil looked amazed by her response.

"This woman saw us praying and is a Christian. Her name is Elizabeth. She's part of a tiny Christian fellowship down the mountain. She treks up here during the week to manage the lodge."

Jeff was shocked. "I didn't know there were any churches around here."

Emil grinned. "There are just a few."

Immediately, Jeff remembered the verse about the glory of God. All it would take was people like Kunda and this woman, and the glory would spread. Jeff was overwhelmed by the thought.

Emil went on. "She wants to pray with us."

Everyone nodded. For the next hour, they prayed for the kids to be found and for the glory of God to fall on Nepal. After seeing the love of Jesus in Elizabeth's eyes, Jeff had new hope for this nation.

❖❖❖❖❖❖❖

Jeff awoke with a start on Tuesday morning. He looked at his watch. It was 5:45 a.m. He remembered they had to get up early and search the town, so he fought the desire to go back to sleep. Pondering what had happened the night before, Jeff knew it was no accident they had come to this lodge. He believed that God's glory really would fill Nepal. Then he remembered that Tenzing and Chandra were still missing and felt conflicted with feelings of both hope and despair.

The sound of the alarm jolted Jeff back awake. Pulling himself out of his sleeping bag, he looked over at Emil, who was packing up. "What should we do now?"

"Hope for a miracle."

Jeff agreed. Putting on his boots, he headed for the common bathroom, then to breakfast. Soon everyone joined him.

"I couldn't get those kids off my mind," Nima said. "I didn't sleep at all."

"It doesn't look too hopeful," Jeff worried. "I feel so empty inside. We should have watched those kids while they slept."

"We can't change that now," Emil said. "We need a new plan. Let's meet for a few minutes and then start the search. It would probably be a good idea to question the police first."

Everyone nodded glumly.

A few minutes later, the front door opened. Jeff watched as a policeman dressed in a green uniform walked in and talked to Elizabeth. Finally, the policeman headed straight toward Emil. Emil looked scared, and Jeff wondered if Goray had managed to convince the police that Emil was a kidnapper.

A confused look crossed Emil's face. "He's asking me if I know Warren Russell."

Jeff couldn't believe his ears. "How does he know about Warren?"

Emil spent a few more minutes talking with the policeman. Then he turned to the team again. "Warren is staying at a lodge in town. The police are holding him for questioning, and they want us to go with them to the lodge for questioning, too."

The shocked team followed the policeman to another trekking lodge. Walking inside the lodge, Jeff almost forget his confusion in his happiness to see Warren approaching them.

"How did you get here?" Jeff asked.

Warren walked over without a limp. "After two days of treatment in Pokhara, the doctor released me. I hired a guide and arrived last night. I searched the town for you, but you hadn't arrived. When it got dark and you hadn't arrived, I got a room at the lodge."

Jeff was thrilled to see Warren's ankle healed.

"You won't believe what happened this morning," Warren said. "And you'll never believe who I ran into."

"Goray," K.J. guessed.

"Nope. Early this morning, I was awakened by a screaming child. I had heard that little voice before."

"Go on," Jeff urged.

"As I walked down the hall to investigate, I saw a door that was slightly open, so I looked inside. And inside were Chandra and Tenzing."

Jeff was stunned.

"Were they by themselves?" Mindy probed.

"No," Warren said. "Shawn and Jay were with them, but they hadn't seen me yet."

"I knew those guys were up to something," K.J. said. "Where are they?"

"Wait a minute," Warren said. "Let me finish my story. I was about to go to the police when Shawn and Jay walked out of their room," he explained.

"Then what happened?" Mindy asked.

"They were glad to see me."

"I'm confused," Jeff said.

"Let me finish."

"Hurry," Mindy begged.

"They explained to me that Goray had tried to talk them into selling the kids in Ghoripani. Shawn and Jay were under the impression that Goray wanted to get the kids to a relative in Kathmandu. But Goray had always intended to sell the kids."

"So Shawn and Jay really were deceived by Goray," K.J. said.

Warren nodded. "Yes. When they got to Ghoripani, they got in a big argument with him over it. Goray went out and got drunk. Then he got into a fight and was arrested. After that, the police discovered that he's been involved in other illegal activity. He'll be in jail for quite a while."

"Where are the kids?" Mindy asked.

"I'm getting there," Warren said, smiling. "Shawn and Jay were planning to take the kids to the police, but then they saw me. I agreed that we should still take them to the police. Shawn and Jay felt so badly about doubting you. Once they saw what a dishonest person Goray was, they realized that a group of kids as determined and compassionate as you couldn't possibly want to harm Tenzing and Chandra. I'm so proud of you for living the gospel in front of these guys."

"Living the gospel? What do you mean?" K.J. questioned.

"I mean that the way you guys acted toward other people really made an impact on Jay and Shawn. They saw that you were determined to help people, and you kept up a good attitude even when things got difficult. Your actions demonstrated God's love and forgiveness."

"I hope so," Jeff said. "And I hope that someday they will realize who the Truth really is."

Mindy was getting impatient. "Where are the kids?"

"The police have them in another room. They're trying to verify our stories. They want to see the adoption papers."

"I want to see Tenzing and Chandra," Mindy said.

"Me, too," Nima cried. "They're my sister and brother. It's time to take them home."

❖❖❖❖❖❖❖❖

Early Christmas morning, Jeff knew he was living in the middle of a miracle. The trekkers were relieved to be back in the warm, cozy apartment in Kathmandu, and Mary Anne was overjoyed to see Tenzing and Chandra. The presents that had been under the beautifully decorated Christmas tree had been torn open, and now Mary Anne was was busy preparing the Christmas breakfast. Jeff was glad she hadn't had any more encounters with the angry relative.

Tenzing was playing with Nima on the floor. Chandra sat in Mindy's lap, smiling calmly. K.J. filmed everything. Ang Fu and Passang watched everyone with great curiosity.

Mindy smiled nonstop. "This is the best Christmas I've ever had."

"You know what's cool," K.J. said, looking at his watch. "We'll still get home in time to enjoy Christmas Day in Los Angeles. We'll gain a whole day flying back."

For once that morning, Mindy quit smiling. "I don't want to leave."

K.J. turned to Warren. "I still don't believe how God worked this all out. I was blown away by what

Shawn and Jay did once they realized the truth about Goray. Jay was so sorry they had helped him. He even asked me some more about Jesus, so we talked and I gave him my Bible to read."

"We'll pray for him," Mindy said.

"We'll pray for both of them," corrected K.J.

"Our flight leaves at 11:30," Warren reminded them. "So make sure all your stuff is packed."

Jeff wanted to memorize the scene. Filled with joy, he watched Emil hold Tenzing. Jeff let the tears flow from his eyes. Looking around the room so warm with love, and so bright with the knowledge of Christ, he wished everyone in Nepal could be there.

Then they would understand the true glory of Christmas.